# *The Visionary*

## PICTURES FROM NORDLAND

# *The Visionary*

## PICTURES FROM NORDLAND

JONAS LIE

*translated from the Norwegian by Jessie Muir*

ÆGYPAN PRESS

From the edition published in 1894 by Hodder Brothers of London.

*The Visionary*
A publication of
ÆGYPAN PRESS

www.aegypan.com

# Preface

Until a few years ago, Norway was an unknown country to most Englishmen. Occasionally a sportsman went there to kill salmon or to shoot reindeer, but the fjords, glaciers, mountains, and waterfalls were quite beyond the reach of any but the most venturesome travelers. Still less was it supposed that Norway possessed a modern school of poets and novelists. Wergeland, Welhaven, Munch, and Moe among the former, Björnson, Ibsen, Kjelland, and Lie among the latter, were, as far as Englishmen were concerned, "to fortune and to fame unknown." All this has been changed; sportsmen now complain that it becomes more difficult every year to hire rivers. Tourists swarm over the country from the Naze to the North Cape. Ibsen's dramas are played in London theaters, and his novels, and those of Björnson and Lie, are read in Germany and in France, as well as in England and America.

These three writers are of nearly the same age. Ibsen was born in 1828, at Skien on the southeastern coast of Norway; Björnson in the Dovrefjeld in 1832; and Lie at Eker, near Drammen, in 1833. Five years after his son's birth, Lie's father was appointed sheriff of Tromsö, which lies within the Arctic Circle, and young Jonas Lauritz Edemil Lie, to give him his full name, spent six of the most impressionable years of his life at that remote port. There he heard from the sailors many strange tales of romantic adventure and of hazardous escape from shipwreck, with the not uncommon result that he wished to be a sailor himself. He was, therefore, sent to the naval school at Fredriksværn; but his defective eyesight proved fatal to the realization of his wish and the idea of a seafaring life had to be given up. He was removed from Fredriksværn to the Latin School at Bergen, and in 1851 entered the University of Christiania, where he made the acquaintance of Ibsen and Björnson. He graduated in law in 1857, and shortly afterwards began to practice at Konsvinger, a little town in Hamar's Stift between Lake Miosen and the frontier of Sweden. Clients were not numerous or profitable at Konsvinger; Lie found time to write for the newspapers and became a frequent contributor to some of the Christiania journals. Meantime, Ibsen and Björnson were becoming famous in Norway, and in 1865 Lie, perhaps in a spirit of emulation, decided to abandon law for literature. His first venture was a volume of poems which appeared in 1866 and was not successful. During the four following years he devoted himself almost exclusively to journalism, working hard and without much reward, but acquiring the pen of a ready writer and obtaining command of a style which has proved serviceable in his subsequent career. In 1870 he published "The Visionary," – "Den Fremsynte" – of which a translation is now, for the first time, offered to English readers. In the following year he revisited Nordland and traveled into Finmark. Having obtained a small traveling pension from the Government, immediately after his journey to Nordland, he sought the greatest contrast he could find in Europe to the scenes of his childhood and started for Rome. For a time he lived in North Germany, then he migrated to Bavaria, spending his winters in Paris. In 1882 he visited Norway for a time, but returned to the continent of Europe. His voluntary exile from his native land ended in the spring of 1893, when he settled at Holskogen, near Christiansund.

"The Visionary" was followed in 1871 by a volume of short stories "Fortoellinger," and during the next year by a larger and more ambitious book, "The Three-master Future," – "Tremasteren Fremtiden" – a realistic sketch of life in the northern harbors of Norway. Two years later "The Pilot and his Wife" – "Lodsen og hans Hustru" – appeared, a book in every respect greatly in advance of its predecessors. Though written almost entirely in an Italian village it has been justly described by an able critic as "one of the saltiest stories ever published." It placed Lie on a higher pedestal than he had ever before occupied, and brought him into line with Ibsen and Björnson. "The Pilot and his Wife" made its author a popular Norwegian writer, and as it has been translated into several European languages – there are, I believe, two English versions – it was the first step towards the wider reputation Lie now enjoys. His next book was hardly a success. Leaving, happily only for a time, Norwegian folk and Norwegian scenes, he attempted, in 1876, a drama in verse, "Faustina Strozzi," the plot of which is derived from an incident in modern Italian history. He returned to Norwegian subjects in "Thomas Ross" and "Adam Schrader," published in 1878 and 1879, which deal with life and manners in Christiania; but even here he was not quite at home and these two novels are not of his best work. "Rutland" and "Go Ahead!" – "Gaa paa!" – are much better, and these two stories of Norwegian life as exhibited in the merchant navy added greatly to Lie's popularity at home.

"The Slave for Life" – "Livsslaven" – 1883, is in a different vein. The plot is strong and the writer shows himself a keen and careful observer of human nature. Without imputing to him any attempt at imitating Ibsen, "The Slave for Life" certainly exhibits that pessimistic view of existence which is at once attractive to many and repulsive to not a few of Ibsen's readers. "The Family of Gilge," – "Familjen paa Gilge" – is of a somewhat similar character. Ethical objections to these stories are, perhaps, superfluous; it must be admitted that both are popular and have added very considerably to Lie's fame. They were followed by "A Whirlpool" – "En Malström" – 1886; "A Wedded Life" – "En Samliv" – 1887; "The Story of a Dressmaker" – "Maisa Jons" – 1888; and by "The Commodore's Daughters" – "Kommandörens Döttre" – 1889, which has enjoyed the good fortune of being translated into English with an introduction by Mr. Edmund Gosse, a most competent Scandinavian scholar. Since 1889 Lie has published "Evil Forces" – "Onde Magter," a volume of poetry, and two collections of shorter stories, "Otte Fortoellinger" and "Trold." He has recently completed another novel, which will shortly appear, and is, it is believed, to be entitled "Niobe." Jonas Lie completed his sixtieth year on the 6th of November last, and this interesting occasion has been celebrated by a festival given in his honor by the students of his old University at Christiania. A special number of *Samtiden* a Norwegian magazine, has also been devoted to a series of articles on his life and literary work.

The present volume, as has already been said, is a translation of Lie's first story. His literary style is at times very colloquial, and his sentences are often of great length, running on for ten, fifteen, or even twenty lines without a full stop. The difficulty of rendering such a mass of words into English prose without sacrificing the meaning, and of maintaining the easy familiarity of the conversation has been fairly overcome by the translator. The story is simple as compared with some of Lie's later productions, but it will always be interesting, not only in itself but as the earliest production of Norway's most popular novelist. Ibsen and Björnson may be better known in England, in America, and on the Continent of Europe, but Jonas Lie is dearer to the Norwegian heart. He has laid the scene of "The Visionary" in Nordland, the home of his childhood, the last district of Norway to receive the faith of Christendom, and even now the abode of superstitions which have survived centuries of Christian teaching. Except along the coast, and there towns and villages are few and far between, Nordland is very sparsely occupied by men of Norwegian birth. Fins and Laplanders wander over the interior during the brief summer, and have, to some extent, intermarried with the Norwegians on the coast, who are chiefly fishermen and sailors. The seafaring life of the people and the slight intermixture of Fin and Lap blood have not tended to lessen their superstitions, and, doubtless, young Lie heard many a strange tale of sea-goblins and land-spirits as he wandered in his boyhood along the quay and in the streets of Tromsö. Many of the impressions he then received have contributed to the tragic interest of "The Visionary." For "The Visionary" is a tragedy in which resistless Fate hurries its victims to destruction. The hero, David Holst, is one of those unhappy beings who seem doomed to a more than ordinary share of the ills of life. He has inherited from his mother at least a tendency to insanity, and he lives in fear of being involved in a terrible catastrophe, from which he only saves himself by strong efforts of will and by the recollection of the lost love of his youth. The awful calamity which overtook him at the very moment his betrothal to Susanna was sanctioned by her father proved, in fact, his salvation, and delivered him from madness, but its effects were never eradicated. Like Hamlet he found the times out of joint; but, instead of contending with them, he patiently submitted to Fate and won for himself, if not absolute peace, at least a certain amount of tranquility. Throughout his life he was subject to visions. In his earliest days the appearance of a lady carrying a white rose marked the near approach of calamity. In later life a vision of his beloved Susanna was sometimes vouchsafed to him, and as he lay on his deathbed she came, after a long interval, as if beckoning him to join her.

The other characters of the story are naturally drawn. David's stern, yet not unkind father; the minister and his wife; the old clerk, and Susanna herself, will soon make themselves known to the reader. The refusal of Susanna to give up David when she learns that his doctor fears he may become insane, and her victory over her father's objections to her engagement, are proofs of Lie's insight into the depth and steadfastness of the love of a good woman. The story of her death, of the bringing home her body in the boat, and of the scene in the death-chamber, are full of pathos, and are told with the simplicity of a great artist.

"The Visionary" is written in the spirit of a true Nordlander, who is ever contrasting life and nature in the south of Norway with life "up there" at home, and with the more varied aspects of nature in Nordland. The vivid description of the great storm are evidently impressions and recollections of actual experience. Before he became an author Lie had often mused

> "On Man, on Nature, and on Human Life,"

and the first results of these musings were given to the world in "The Visionary."

J.A.J.H.

# PART I

# INTRODUCTION

# Introduction

I know many people who have felt the same inclination that sometimes comes over me, to choose bad weather to go out in. They are generally men who have passed from a childhood lived in the open air of the country, to an occupation which entails much sitting still, and for whom the room sometimes seems to become too narrow and confined – or else they are poets. Their recollection and imagination live, more or less unknown to themselves, in a continual longing to get away from the confined air of a room, and the barrack-life of a town.

So one day when the country comes into the town in the shape of a downright storm of wind and rain, which shakes the tiles on the roofs, and now and then flings one after you, while the streets become rivers, and every corner an ambush from which the whirlwind makes a sudden attack upon your umbrella, and, after a more or less prolonged and adroit struggle, tears it, and turns it inside out, until at last you stand with only the stick and the ribs left in your hand – at such a time, it now and then happens that a quiet, dignified civil servant, or business man, instead of sitting at home, as usual, in the afternoon in his comfortable room after the day's toil in the office, says to his wife that he "is sorry he must go out into the town for a little while." And what he unfortunately must go out for is, of course, "business." For little would it become a sedate, grave man, perhaps an alderman, and one of the fathers of the town, to acknowledge, even to himself, that he is childish enough to go and wander about in bad weather, that he only wants to walk down to the quay to see the spray dash over the bitts, and to watch the ships in the harbor playing at shipwreck. He must, of course, have something to do there; if nothing else, at any rate to see "ne quid detrimenti capiat respublica"; that is to say, that the town, whose welfare, in one way or another, it is his business to look after, is not blown down.

The fact is, there is a revolution in the streets – not a political revolution, Heaven preserve him from that – but one which has an attraction for him, because it awakens all his old recollections, and in which, much to his disgrace, he contrives surreptitiously to join, although, in its own way, it too defies all police arrangements, breaks windows, puts out street-lamps, tears the tiles from the house-roofs, damages piers and moorings, and chases police and watchmen into their holes. It is Nature's loud war-cry, in the very midst of the civilized town, to all the recollections of his childhood, to his imagination and his love of Nature; and he obeys it like an old trumpeter's horse that hears the signal of his youth, and instantly leaps the fence.

After an hour or two out in the storm, the fire in his veins is subdued, and home he comes once more a quiet, grave man, carefully puts his stick and galoshes in their accustomed places in the hall, and is pitied by his wife, who has been anxious about him, and is now helping him off with his wet things. Strange to say, he himself, in spite of adverse circumstances, is in capital spirits that evening, and has such a number of things to tell about this storm – everything of course, as becomes the occasion, in the form of anxiety lest damage should be done, or fire break out in the town.

It was in such weather that I – a practicing doctor, and having, as such, good reason, both on my own account and on that of others, for being out at all times of the day or night – one rainy, misty, stormy October afternoon, roamed the streets of Kristiania, finding pleasure in letting the rain dash in my face, while my mackintosh protected the rest of my person.

Darkness had gradually fallen, and the lighted gas-lamps flared in the gusty wind, making me think of the revolving lights on a foggy night out on the coast. Now and again an unfastened door swung open and shut again, with a bang like a minute gun. My inward comment on these occasions was that, even in our nervous times, there must still be an astonishing number of people without nerves; for such bangs thunder through the whole house right up to the garret, as a gust fills the passage, and doors fly open and shut, shut and open; everybody feels the discomfort, but no one will take the trouble to go down and fasten the origin of the evil; the porter is out in the town, and as long as he is away the inmates must put up with an absence of all domestic comfort.

It was just such an unfastened, unweariedly banging door that led to what I have to relate.

As I passed it, I heard a voice, which seemed familiar to me, an old beloved voice – though at first I could not recall where I had heard it – calling impatiently to the porter. It was on the subject of the banging door. The man was evidently the only nervous individual in that house; at any rate, the porter was not, for he appeared to be quite wanting in feeling both for his door and for the man who had interested himself in it, and was now fumbling in vain with a latchkey, which did not appear to fit.

At last the porter came out of his subterranean hole, and it was during a little altercation between the now placable and gentle voice, sorry for its previous irritability, and the growling porter, that with all the power of an awakened recollection I recognized my old friend of student-days, David Holst, with whom I had lived three of the richest years of my youth.

"If that is you, David, you must let me in before you lock the door!" I cried, just as I should have done in the good old days, twenty years before.

The door opened wide, and a warm shake of the hand from the dark advancing form, told me that he had not needed to search so long through the chambers of his memory as I, but had recognized me at once.

"Follow me!" were his only words, and then we mounted silently, he in front and I behind, up the dark stairs, one, two, three floors and one considerably narrower flight above. There he took my hand to guide me – a very necessary proceeding, for, as far as I could make out, the way led across a dark loft, hung with clothes-lines. He told me, too, to bend my head.

As I mounted I drew my own conclusions. His hand – I remembered that in old days he used to be rather proud of it – was damp, perhaps with mental agitation, and he sometimes stopped as if to take breath. The narrow garret-stairs whispered to me too, that my friend David, who in his time had given promise of good abilities, could not have made great use of them for his own worldly advancement.

He opened a door and bade me go in first.

Upon a table stood a lamp, whose shade concentrated the light round its foot, in a circle of scarcely more than half a yard's radius, upon an inkstand and papers which lay there, leaving the ends of the table in apparent darkness. Behind the table was what looked like a black grave, which, however, when the eye became accustomed to the abrupt transition from light to shadow, revealed itself as a sofa, before which stood an almost correspondingly long, painted, wooden table with square ends.

When two old friends meet in such a way, there is often, under their frank manner, a secret shyness to overcome; for there is a layer of the different experiences of many years that has to be cleared away.

After a short pause, my friend, as if with a sudden resolve, went quickly up to the table and took the shade off the lamp, so that the whole room became light.

"You see," said he, "things are just the same with me as in the old days, only that there are now two garret windows instead of one, a few more shelves with books, and a rather better monthly salary, which I get by combining a teachership in one of the lower-class schools here, with an easy post on a daily paper. It is all I need, you see. I moved here from Bergen this spring, and ought properly to have paid you a call, but have not yet managed it; when I have seen you in the street, you have always looked as if you were too much taken up with your practice. But now that I have you in my den, we will have a chat about old times, and what you are doing. Take off your coat, while I go down and see about getting some toddy made." Whereupon he replaced the lamp shade, and disappeared through the doorway.

My friend's somewhat forced introductory speech did not seem natural to me; it was as though, in his ready confidence, he were regulated rather by my circumstances than by his own, and the whole thing gave me the impression that at the outset he would parry all unnecessary questions.

As yet I, at least, had not said a word; indeed, I had not seen more of my friend than a brief glimpse of his face, as he turned towards the lamp and replaced the shade. Still I recognized, in spite of the difference in age, the same thin, delicate, pale face, which, in the old days, would sometimes assume such a beautiful, melancholy expression – it was with that he was always photographed in my memory – but the features had now acquired a striking sharpness, and in the quick glance I caught there was an expression, both suffering and searching, which made me indescribably sad. I have seen sick people look at me in the same way, when they were afraid they were to be operated upon; and I thought I now understood at any rate this much, that what wanted operating on here was my friend's confidence, and this would require all my dexterity.

I was once the most confiding fellow under the sun; but since I became a doctor and saw what people really are, I have become thoroughly suspicious; for there is nothing in the whole world you may not have to presuppose, even with the best of mortals, if you do not want to be misled as to the cause of their disease. I suspect everybody and everything, even, as the reader has seen above, those sedate men who go out in stormy weather. An Indian does not steal more unperceived and noiselessly through a primeval forest than I, when necessary, into my patient's confidence; and my friend David had all at once become my patient. He would scarcely succeed in deceiving *me* any longer with his talk about "old days" and a glass of punch in his "unchanged student's den."

My first stratagem was now hastily to continue the inspection of the room, which my friend had somewhat cursorily allowed me to begin. I took the lamp and began to look about me.

Under the sloping ceiling, against the wall opposite the sofa, was the bed, with a little round table beside it. On some bookshelves, which stood on the floor against the wall in the corner at the foot of the bed, I recognized Henrik Wergeland's bust, even more defective about the chin and nose than in my time, and now, in addition, blind in one eye; he had fared almost as badly as the old pipe I used to smoke, which I recognized again, in spite of its being cut and hacked in every direction. For my friend had a habit of cutting marks in it while he sat smoking, now and then throwing a word into the conversation to keep it going, just as one throws fuel on a fire – it was the spirit of the conversation, and that something should be said, rather than the thought itself, he cared about. When sitting thus, his face often wore a melancholy, peaceful expression, as if he were smiling at something beautiful we others did not see.

Between the bed and the shelves I discovered some bottles, ordinary spirit bottles, and the suspicion flashed like lightning through my mind – I have, as I said, become suspicion personified, not naturally, but through disappointment – that my friend was perhaps given to drink.

I put the lamp down upon the floor. In one bottle was ink, in the second paraffin, and in the third, a smaller one, cod-liver oil, which he probably took for his chest.

I remembered his clammy hand, his stopping, and heavy breathing on the stairs, and I felt thoroughly ashamed that I could have been such a wretch as to think the dear friend, I might also say ideal, of my youth, was no better than any scamp in vulgar life, who positively ought to be suspected.

I offered him, in silence, a penitent apology, while I read over the titles on the backs of the books, recognizing one and another. These shelves seemed to be the bookshelves of his student days. I drew out a thick volume, old "Saxo Grammaticus," which I remembered to have bought at an auction, and presented to him; but now I found something quite different to think about.

It happened with me as with a man who draws out a brick and suddenly finds a secret passage – I all at once felt myself at the entrance to my friend's secret, though, as yet, only before a deep, dark room through which my imagination might wander, but which I could not really see, unless my friend himself held the light for me.

What thus attracted my attention and riveted my thought and recollection to the spot, was no hole, but the head of a violin, with a dusty neck, and a tangle of strings about the screws which was stuck up at the back of the shelf. The fourth string hung loosely down; the over-stretched, broken first had curled up, and under the two whole strings the bridge lay flat, as I ascertained by taking several books out of the row and feeling for it. I examined the violin, which I could easily remove, as carefully as if I had found a friend ill and starving; there was an unmended crack in the body. Enchained by old memories, I could not help falling into a very sad frame of mind.

I put the books on the shelves again, replaced the lamp on the table, and sat myself on the sofa, where puffing away at the pipe (I found on it among others my own initials, cut by myself) I gave myself up to reflections, which I will here impart to the reader even at the risk of his thinking my friend is rather a long time getting the punch. Through these reflections he will stand before the reader, as he did before my mind's eye in the light of youthful recollections, and as the reader must know him, if he will understand him.

Our acquaintance as students arose naturally from the fact that we were both from Nordland. He was three or four years older than I, and his being the trusted though anonymous theatrical reviewer on the H—— paper, was enough of itself to give him, in my eyes, an official superiority, before which I bowed.

But what worked still more strongly upon my youthful imagination was his manner. There was something unusually noble about his slender figure and his delicate, oval-shaped, earnest face, with the high forehead and the heavy masses of dark, curly hair on the temples. His strongly-marked eyebrows and a decided Roman nose drew one's attention away from his eyes, which were light blue, and more in keeping with his pale and beardless face than with his more energetic features. But yet it was his eyes that gave one the first impression of him. I learned later to read his features differently, and to see that in them was reflected the meeting of the currents of that twofold nature by which his life was gradually crushed out.

A sweet smile when he talked and a reserved manner gave him a distinguished air, which at any rate impressed me greatly. He was the only student I knew who did not wear a student's cap; he used to wear a flat blue sailor's cap with a short peak, which suited him very well. When he became eager, as might happen in a dispute – for he was a great logician, though it was only his intellect that took part in a discussion, and never, as far as I could see, his heart or his deeper feelings – his voice would give way; it became overstrained and harsh, as if from a weak chest. Such encounters always told upon him, and left him in irritable restlessness for some time after.

One of his peculiarities was that he sometimes went on walking tours of several days out in the country, both in summer and winter. Companionship he would never hear of. Had he wished for it, he would have asked me I knew, and therefore I never thought of forcing myself upon him.

On these occasions he would set off without a knapsack; I noticed this once when I happened to be roaming in the fields two or three miles[*] from a town, where I had gone on a visit. When he came home again, he would be in capital spirits, but before setting out he was always so silent and melancholy that I had to sustain nearly the whole burden of the conversation. He used to have periods of low spirits.

One indication of these moods was his manner in playing on the violin I had now found with broken strings, at the back of his bookshelf. As it lay there, it recalled the incidents of twenty years ago.

This violin he once held in high esteem; it had the place of honor on his wall, with the bow beside it. It had been left him by a friend, an old clerk,[†] at his home up in the north, who had taught him to play, and had evidently been one of those musical geniuses who are never fully appreciated in this world.

David loved to give play to his fancy, not only upon this violin – he had a good ear, and had learnt not a little – but also about it: where it really came from, and how old it might be? He would exceedingly have liked an indistinct mark inside to mean that it was "possibly a Cremona"; it was one of his weak points, and this room for conjecture was evidently, in his eyes, one of the excellences of the violin.

David had a small collection of what he called classical music, long compositions which he played from the notes. They were not much to my fancy, and always struck me as being of a piece with what was strange in his manner when he posed as a logician. When he played them it was more like severe, mental, school exercise than anything his heart was in; and he played as correctly as he argued or wrote.

The times when classical music and critical conversations ruled in his room, were certainly those in which he felt his mind most in balance. He was less hearty in manner then, even towards me.

But then would come times when the music-stand would remain in the corner. He would sit for a long time looking straight before him, as if lost in thought, and then give expression to his feeling, on his violin, in all kinds of fantasies, which pleased my uncultivated ear far more

* A Norwegian mile is about seven English miles.

† Norw. "klokker," almost answering to the Scotch precentor, but a klokker, in addition to leading the singing in church, has to read the opening prayer and to assist the priest in putting on his vestments.

than his so-called classical music.

He sometimes played a variety of small pieces, and then gradually sank into his own peculiar minor strain, and sometimes into a wonderfully sad melody. I very seldom heard him play anything right through, and then always in a kind of self-forgetfulness. At such times, I had a feeling that he was confiding to me something beautiful that he had lost, and over which he could never cease to mourn.

At a later period of our friendship he became, as I have said, more irregular in his habits, and was seldom to be found at home; he would sometimes talk ironically about his comrades, the professors and things in general, and his sarcasm was almost biting.

I was privileged to take my friend's key, and go into his room, even when he was not at home. If his violin hung uncared for, I knew that something was wrong, and that his own condition answered to that of his instrument. The first thing he did, when all was right again, was carefully to put it in order.

But never during those times had I seen his treasure so badly treated and neglected as when twenty years later, I found it again, dusty and cracked at the back of the bookshelf. The reader will now be able to understand how sorrowful were the reflections it aroused, and how it led me to suspect the story of a joyless life; and I trust he will forgive me for having taken him so far from David Holst's room – where I sat and waited for my friend to come with the punch – into the land of my youthful recollections. For three years we had been together almost daily. After that David had to go out as tutor, and our ways parted, as they so often do in this life.

And this evening we had met again.

There was a jingling in the passage, and immediately after David Holst carefully opened the door for a servant-girl, who brought in a steaming jug of hot water and other requisites for punch, which were most welcome to a man who had been out several hours in the wind and rain, as I had that very afternoon.

David found me installed on the sofa with his pipe in my mouth and his slippers on my feet, just as he would have done in the old days, and this I reckoned as one of my cunning artifices; for with these passes, his pipe and slippers, I reinstated myself, without more ado, on the old friendly footing. I felt like a general who is fortunate enough to open the campaign by occupying a whole province.

In default of his accustomed place on the sofa, David drew a chair up to the table and sat down opposite to me, with the punch tray between us.

We were now once more on the banks of the same river of delight, in which we had so often bathed and tumbled in our youth; but now we both approached it more carefully.

In the course of conversation, he often leaned over towards me, as if listening, and in this way his head came within the region of the lamp's bright light. I then noticed that his hair was much thinner, and sprinkled rather plentifully with grey, and that the perspiration stood in beads on his no longer unwrinkled brow. His pallid, sharp-featured face, and a strange brilliancy in his eyes, told me that either his physical or his mental being hid an underground fire, perhaps no longer quenchable. Thinking from his repeated fits of coughing, that his bending over towards me arose quite as much from the fact that he was tired and was trying to rest against the edge of the table, as from his interest in the conversation, I determined to enter at once upon the question of the state of his health, and thus put myself in possession of yet another important outwork of his confidence.

I rose suddenly, determined and serious, and said that, as an experienced doctor, I unfortunately saw that he was ill in no such slight degree as he perhaps thought, and that, as he was evidently weak and languid – as the drops of perspiration on his forehead showed – he must, at any rate, at once seat himself on the comfortable sofa I had hitherto occupied.

He acknowledged that going twice downstairs had been rather too much for him – the first time he had only gone down to put an end to the uncomfortable draft through the house – and willingly took his place on the sofa at my desire.

It was his chest, he said. By the help of the stethoscope, I found that this was only too true. His chest, indeed, was in such a condition that it was only a question of gaining time, not of saving life; for one lung was entirely gone, and the other seriously affected.

During the remainder of the evening, both he and I felt ourselves re-established on the old footing, my authority as doctor now giving me a slight superiority.

At nine o'clock, I declared that he must go to bed, and I told him that the next morning I intended to come again, and prescribe what was needful. I heard he was not to be at school before eleven: until that hour he promised me not to go out.

When I came home, I found my wife in great anxiety about me. She could not conceive how a sensible man, and a doctor into the bargain, who gave others such good advice, could be out more than was necessary in such dreadful weather; and I had been out in it the whole time since dinner.

There was nothing to be said to this, and I only considered, while she talked, how I could best win her over to the cause which I now had at heart. My wife had not the slightest acquaintance with my dying friend, and, if I knew her aright, might even feel hurt when I told her that he had, in a way, possessed my affection before I knew her.

Things turned out as I foresaw; for it was only after a rather doubtful pause that she came up to me, and said that my best friend should of course be dear to her.

And from that moment no one could have been more helpful than she. Whatever she undertakes, she always does thoroughly, and she settled that very evening how the matter should be arranged.

At ten the next morning I was up in my friend's room with my wife, and I introduced her to him, saying that she wished to be regarded as an old friend like myself. I told him, as consolingly as I could – but when I said it, my wife looked away – that his illness absolutely required that he should put himself under treatment for six months, until the warm weather came and completed his cure, and that I hoped he would consent to let me arrange matters at the school for him.

He was evidently both surprised and touched. Life had not offered him friendship, he said; he was so little used to accept it, even when it came to him as true and good as this was. After a little parleying, he surrendered at discretion to my wife, who never liked being defeated.

He would not, however, move to our house, as I suggested, for he had a fondness for this room, and, as he frankly said, he would not feel happy if obligations of a pecuniary nature were introduced into the matter.

From this time I visited him as a rule every morning, and generally had a little chat about different things in the town which I thought might interest, or at any rate divert him.

My wife treated him in her own way. Contrary to what I had been a little afraid of, she carried out no radical revolution in his housekeeping arrangements. That the servant-girl had her reasons for coming up to him so often, and that every day she waited in fear and trembling my wife's quiet inspection whether the room were properly dusted and in order, he could have no suspicion.

The only thing that my wife openly effected, was the sending of all kinds of strengthening food. One of the children often went with the maid who took these, and it sometimes amused and entertained him, to keep the child with him for a while.

This new and unaccustomed state of affairs seemed at first to divert him; but in the course of a month he began to be depressed again. Our visits evidently troubled him, and, for this reason, were discontinued for a time. He spent almost the whole day on the sofa at the dark end of the room.

One evening the girl said she had heard a sound as of crying and sobbing in his room, so she did not go in, but remained standing outside. A little while after it seemed to her as if he were praying earnestly, but she did not understand the words. The next evening she heard him playing a soft melody, as if on a violin which did not give a clear sound.

The following morning when I came to him his mood was entirely changed, and to my surprise I saw that his violin, dusted and with strings in order, but still cracked, hung on the wall with the bow beside it. On the table, by the bed, I noticed too an old Bible that I had never before seen, probably because this treasure had always been kept in his drawer as a sacred thing.

He looked more languid and worn out than usual; but his face wore a beatified expression, as of a man who had wrestled with his fate, and had won rest and resignation.

If possible, he said, he would like to speak to my wife that same morning; but he would rather talk with me at once, and so I must sit down for a little while.

With a smile – that same quiet, sweet, mysterious smile of his that I knew so well, but which now seemed no longer to shun observation – he turned to me saying, as he laid his hand on my shoulder and looked into my face:

"My dear, kind Frederick! I know for certain, though I cannot tell you why, that I shall not live to see the spring again. What is wanting neither you nor anyone else can give me, only God; but of all men you have been the kindest to me, and your friendship has reached farther than you would ever imagine. You have a right to know him who has been your friend. When I am gone – and that will undoubtedly be this winter, perhaps sooner than you, judging from my condition, think – you will find some memoranda in my drawer; they are the history of my early youth, but uneventful as that was, it has had its effect upon my whole life. It will tell you that the world has been sad, very sad for me, and that I am as glad as an escaped bird to leave it."

"There was a time," he added after some hesitation, "when I wished to be buried in a churchyard up in Nordland; but now I think that the place does not make any difference, and that one can rest just as peacefully down here."

Saying which, he pressed my hand, and asked me to go for my wife.

When she came, she was surprised to see him brighter and in better spirits than she had ever thought he could be. He wanted, he said, to ask a favor of her. It was a whim of his; but, if he should be called away, she must promise him to plant a wild rose upon his grave next spring.

My wife understood how sad the request was when I told her what had already passed; for David had looked so confident and bright when he was talking to her, that the sorrowful element was absent.

My friend's prophecy about himself proved to be only too true. Though his mood grew constantly brighter, so that he sometimes even had a gleam of the joy of living, his illness went in the opposite direction, always toward the worst.

One day I found him lying and watching from his bed – where he now spent nearly the whole day – my little Anton, who had "made a steamboat" out of his old violin-case – of which the lid was gone – and was traveling with it on the floor, touching at foreign ports. When I came up to the bed, David told me, smiling, that he had been at home in Nordland playing on the beach again.

My wife had, meantime, become more and more his sick-nurse. She was with him two or three times a day, and sat at his bedside. He often held her hand, or asked her to read him something out of his old Bible. The portions he chose were generally those in which the Old Testament speaks of love and lovers. He dwelt especially on the story of Jacob and Rachel.

My wife, who had now become very fond of him, confided to me one day that she was sure she knew what my friend was suffering from; it was certainly nothing but unrequited love.

She had never thought anyone could look so touchingly beautiful as he did, when death was near. When he lay still and smiled, it was as though he were thinking of a tryst he should go to, as soon as he had done with us here on earth.

One evening he asked my wife to sit with him. At nine o'clock a message came for me; but when I got there, he was gone.

He had asked my wife to read to him, for the first time, a part of Solomon's Song, where she found an old mark in his Bible. It was the second chapter, in which both the bride and the bridegroom speak, and which begins: "I am the rose of Sharon, and the lily of the valley"; and ends: "Until the day break, and the shadows flee away, turn, my beloved, and be thou like a roe or a young hart upon the mountains of Bether."

He had asked her to read it a second time, but during the reading he had quietly fallen asleep.

And there he lay, beautiful in death, with a peaceful smile, as though he were greeting just such a grove, on the other side of the mountains of Bether.

Next summer there stood a wooden cross, and a blooming, wild briar-rose, on a grave in one of the churchyards of the town. There rests my friend David Holst.

As a beginning of the story of my friend's life, I found, laid aside, a section, part of which seems to have been added at a riper age. It shows with what strong ties nature had bound him to his home, and with what affection he clung to it.

# PART II

## NORDLAND AND NORDLANDERS

# *Nordland and Nordlanders*

In so far as a man like myself, who lives in such a sad reality, dare talk of illusions – how great, and what a number of illusions I have had shattered, during the two or three years since I left my home in Nordland, and became a student; how grey and colorless is the world down here, how small and mean, compared with what I had imagined it as regards both men and conditions of life!

This afternoon, I was out fishing in the fjord with some friends; of course they all enjoyed themselves – and I pretended that I did. No, I did not enjoy myself! We sat in a flat-bottomed, broad, ugly boat, that they called a "pram," a contrivance resembling a washtub, and fished the whole afternoon in muddy water a few feet deep, with a fine line, catching altogether seven whiting – and then rowed quite satisfied to land! I felt nearly sick; for the whole of life down here seems to me like this pram, without a keel, by which to shape a course, without a sail, which one cannot even fancy could be properly set in such a boat, without rough weather, which it could not stand, and like this muddy, grey, waveless sea outside the town, with only a few small whiting in it. Life here has nothing else to offer than such small whiting.

While the others talked, I sat and thought of a fishing expedition when *she* was with me, out among the Vætte Rocks at home, in our little six-oared boat – what a different kind of day, what a different kind of boat, what a different experience! Yes, how unromantic, poor and grey, life is down here among the rich, loamy, corn-producing hills, or on the fjord of the capital, sooty with steamboat smoke, or even in the town itself, compared with that at home! But if I uttered this aloud, how these superior people would open their eyes!

They talk here of fishing, and are pleased with a few poor cod and whiting. A Nordlander understands by fishing a haul of a thousand fish; he thinks of the millions of Lofoten and Finmark, and of an overwhelming variety of species, of whales, spouting through the sounds, and driving great shoals of fish before them, as well as of the very smallest creatures of the deep. The only fish that I know down here worth noticing – and I always look at them whenever I come across them – are the gold and silver fish, that you keep in a glass-bowl, just as you keep a canary in a cage: but then they are from another fairyland in the south.

When a Nordlander speaks of birds he does not mean as they do here, only a head or two of game, but an aërial throng of winged creatures, rippling through the sky, flying round the rocks, like white foam, or descending like a snowstorm on their nesting-places; he thinks of eider-duck, guillemot, diver and oyster-catcher swimming in fjord and sound, or sitting upon the rocks; of gulls, ospreys and eagles, hunting in the air; of the eagle-owl, hooting weirdly at night in the mountain-clefts – in short, he means a whole world of birds, and has a little difficulty in confining his ideas to the poor capercailzie, surprised and killed by a sportsman in the midst of a love-frolic, when the sun is rising over the pine-clad hills.

Instead of the fruit-gardens here, he has the miles of cloudberry moors at home. Instead of a poor, uniform shore with nothing but mussels, he remembers a grand beach strewn with myriads of marvelously tinted shells.

All natural conditions are intensified in Nordland, and are far more powerfully contrasted than in the south of Norway. Nordland is a boundless stone-grey waste, as it was in primæval times before man began to build, but in the midst of this there are also countless natural treasures; it has a sun and a summer glory, whose day is not twelve hours only, but an uninterrupted period of three months, during which, in many places, one must wear a mask as protection against the swarms of mosquitoes; but, on the other hand, the night is a time of darkness and horror, lasting nine months. Everything there is on a gigantic scale without the gradual transitions between extremes, upon which the quiet life here in the south is built; in other words, there are more occasions for fancy, adventure and chance, than for calm reasoning, and quiet activity with certain results.

A Nordlander, therefore, down here, is at first apt to feel like Gulliver, who has come to Lilliput, and, on the whole, does not get on well among the inhabitants, until he has screwed down his old customary ideas to the simple proportions of their insignificant life; in short, until he has taught himself to use his intellect, instead of his fancy.

The Lap on snow-shoes with his reindeer, the Fin, the Russian, not to mention the constantly moving Nordlander himself, who, though slow on land, is quick in his boat – are all undeniably far more interesting people than the dull southern rustic, whose imagination reaches scarcely farther than his own field, or to wondering whereabouts in the pasture he must go to fetch his horse.

When Southerners talk about storms and waves, they mean a little bit of a storm and rough sea in the Kristiania Fjord, which can even do a little damage in the harbor; and they consider it deeply affecting when a clumsy boatman is drowned. A storm suggests something very different to my mind: a sudden down rushing wind from the mountains, which carries away houses – for which reason they are secured with ropes at home; waves from the Arctic Sea, which bury high rocks and islands in foam, and roll ground-seas of innumerable fathoms' depth, so that vessels are suddenly dashed to pieces in the middle of the ocean; crowds of brave men sailing for their very lives before the wind, and not for their lives only, but also to save the dearly-won cargo for the sake of those at home, and, even in deadly peril, trying to lend a hand to a capsized comrade; I think of the shipwreck of countless boats and vessels on a winter evening, in the hollows of the foaming waves. It would, for once, be worth while to see such waves (usually three in succession, and the last the worst) advancing with their crests higher than the custom-house roof, and bearing on their shoulders a yacht, which has to be run ashore, rushing into Kristiania's peaceful little harbor, carrying ships up with them into the town, and followed by correspondingly fierce bursts of wind, lifting off the very roofs. If they came, I know well it would be *me* they wanted, *me* the poor visionary, hidden away in the civilization of the town, who, they consider, belongs to them; and I think a moment after the terror I should greet them as friends from home, although they came bearing death and destruction on their wings. They would, for once, show to all this civilized littleness the terrible grandeur and greatness of the mighty ocean, and flavor the insipidity of the town with a little sea-salt terror. I should like to see a whale squeezed in between Prince's Street and Custom-house Street, glaring at a family on the upper floor, or the fine, gold-laced policemen trying to bring into court a stranded sea-goblin. I should like, too, to see the town's theatrical reviewers, who are accustomed to see "Haupt und Statsaction" in vaudevilles twice a week, stand with their eye-glasses to their eyes, before such a play, which, without more ado, would swamp all their critical ideas and inkstands, and show them death and horror in real downright earnest.

How such a reviewer would grow in ability to understand what is imposing and powerful in a poetical composition, and in the desires it awakens, if he only once in his life had seen the "Horseman,"* on a

* A remarkable mountain in Nordland.

stormy day, with its height of 1700 feet, riding southwards out in the surf, while his cloak fluttered from his shoulder towards the north, and, besides the giant himself in his might, had seen, in prefect illusion, the horse's head, his ear, his neck, his snaffle and his majestic chest.

It is up in the north that northern popular imagination, from the time of the myths, has laid the home of a whole army of wickedness; there the Fin folk have practiced their magic arts, and woven their spells; and there by the dark, wintry-grey breakers of the Arctic Sea, live yet the ancient gods of evil, driven out to earth's farthest limits, those demoniacal, terrible, half-formless powers of darkness, with whom the Aases fought, but St. Olaf, with his victorious, dazzling, cross-hilt sword, "turned to stock and stone."

That which can so easily be put aside as superstition, when one is sitting safely in the middle of civilization – and yet still lives as a natural power in the people – is represented, on the whole, in pigmy proportions in the south. Here they have a little terror of small hobgoblins, good-natured fairies, a love-sick river-sprite, and so forth, beings who with us in the north, almost go about our houses like superstition's tame domestic animals. You have there, too, good-natured elves, who carry on their peaceful boating and coasting trade invisibly among the people. But then, in addition, natural terror creates a whole host of wicked demons, who draw people with an irresistible power, the ghosts of drowned men, who have not had Christian burial, mountain ogres, the sea-sprite, who rows in a half boat, and shrieks horribly on the fjords on winter nights. Many who really were in danger have let their chance of safety go for fear of him, and the visionaries can actually see him.

But if Nature's great power, brooding with crushing weight over life on this wintry, surf-beat, iron-bound coast, which lies in twilight for nine months, and for three of these altogether loses the sun, creates a terror of darkness in the mind, yet the north also possesses in the same extreme the exactly opposite character, a warm, sunny, summer nature, clear-aired, heavily scented, rich with the changing beauty of countless colors; in which objects at ten or twelve miles' distance across the sea-mirror, seem to approach within speaking-distance; in which the mountains clothe themselves with brownish green grass to the very top – in Lofoten to a height of 2000 feet – in which the small birch woods wreathe themselves up on the slopes and ravines, like white, sixteen-year-old maidens at play; in which too the air is laden, as in no other place, with the scent of the growing strawberries and raspberries there, and when the day is so hot, that you are compelled to walk in shirt-sleeves, and you are longing to bathe in the rippling sea, always saturated with sunshine, and perfectly clear to the very bottom.

The powerful aroma and bright color of things growing there, have been attributed by the learned to the strong light that fills the atmosphere, when the sun is above the horizon uninterruptedly the whole twenty-four hours. And in no other place can such deliciously flavored strawberries or raspberries, nor such fragrant birch-boughs, be gathered as in Nordland.

If there is a home for a wonderfully beautiful idyll, it must be in the fjord-valleys of Nordland in the summertime. It is as though the sun kisses Nature all the more lovingly, because he knows how short a time they have to be together, and as if they both, for the time, try to forget that they must part so soon. Then the hill grows green as if by a sudden miracle, and the bluebell, the dandelion, the buttercup, the dog-daisy, the wild rose, the raspberry and the strawberry spring up in lavish abundance, by every brook, on every hillock, on every mountain-slope; then hundreds of insects hum in the grass as in a tropical land; then cows, horses, and sheep are driven up the hills and the mountainsides, while the Fin from the highlands comes down into the valley with his reindeer and waters them in the river; then the cloudberry moors lie reddening for many a mile inland; then there is quiet, sunny peace in every cottage, where the fisherman is now sitting at home with his family, putting his tackle in order for the winter fishing; for in Nordland the summer is more beautiful than in any other place, and there is an idyllic gladness and peace over Nature, which is to be found nowhere else.

The Nordlander, too, has a touch of Nature's caressing softness in his character; when he can manage it, he is fond of living and dressing well, and lodging comfortably; with regard to delicacies, he is a thorough epicure. Cod's tongue, young ptarmigan, reindeer-marrow, salted haddock, trout, salmon and all kinds of the best salt-water fish, appropriately served with liver and roe, nourishing reindeer-meat and a variety of game are, like the fresh-flavored cloudberries, only everyday dishes to him. And the Fin as well as the Nordland plebeian is also childishly fond of all sweet things, and his "syrup and porridge" are widely known.

Brought up in the midst of a nature so rich in contrasts and possibilities, and amidst scenes of the utmost variety, from the wildest grandeur to the tenderest beauty, charm and fascination, the Nordlander is, as a rule, clever and bright, often indeed brilliant and imaginative. Impressionable as he is, he yields easily to the impulse of the moment. If there is sunshine in your face, there is sure to be sunshine in his. But you must not be mistaken in him, and take his good nature for perfect simplicity – as is often done here in the south. Deep in his soul there lurks a silent suspicion, unknown even to himself, he is always like a watchful sea-fowl that dives at the flash of the gun, and before the bullet has had time to strike the spot where it just now lay on the water. He has been used from childhood to think of the unexpected, the possibility of all possible things in Nature, as a sword hanging over every peaceful, quiet hour, and he generally carries this instinct with him in his intercourse with his fellow-creatures. While you are talking to him, he may dive into his mind like the sea-fowl, but you do not suspect it, and are not therefore disconcerted. This introspection may occur while he has tears in his eyes, and in moments when he is most deeply affected – it is his nature, and he will always retain a dash of it, even when he has moved, with all his belongings, from natural into civilized surroundings. He eludes you, steals, with his imagination and his watchful suspicion, in, among, and around your thoughts; indeed, if he is a really talented Nordlander – I am too dull and disinterested to be able to do it – I believe that, without your suspecting it, he can go, with his hands in his pockets, right through your mind, in at your forehead, and out at the back of your head. He would be invaluable as a detective or a diplomatist, if only he had more strength of character, and succumbed with less childish weakness to the influence of the moment; but these are unfortunately his weak points. I am speaking now of the strong trait in the national character as it shows itself in the more conspicuous natures, and would not be misunderstood to mean that men of character are not to be found in Nordland too – many a time, perhaps oftener than elsewhere, they are hardened into something grand.

In a native Nordland family there will generally be found – such, at least, is my belief – some drops of Fin blood. It has been remarked elsewhere that in the Sagas, when the greatest peasant races in Halgoland were spoken of as descended from half-trolls, or mountain-ogres, this only meant Finnish descent. Our royal families were of Finnish extraction, and Fin was a good-sounding name borne by the greatest men in the land – for instance, Fin Arnesen.* Harald Haarfager and Erik Blodöxe both married Fin maidens. The mystic sense-affecting influence which has been ascribed to them, was only the erotic expression of the great national connection between the two differently derived elements; the fair-haired, blue-eyed, larger-minded and quieter Norwegian, and the dark, brown-eyed Fin, quick of thought, rich in fancy, filled with the mysticism of nature, but down-trodden and weak in character. The Fin, to this very day, goes as it were on snow-shoes and sings minor strains, while many a Norwegian, in his pride of race, little suspects that he has any connection with that despised people.

---

* One of Olaf the Holy's most trusted men.

There is also, in my experience, a great difference in our national character, which depends upon whether the crossing has taken place with the weak Laplander, or with the well-grown, strong, bold Fin. It makes a difference in temperament, as great as between minor and major in the same piece of music. That touch of rich color in our nation, of which the poet Wergeland's endless wealth of imagery and flight beyond logic are a representation, is certainly Finnish – at any rate, there is very little of it in our old Sagas. And it can be understood from this, what grandeur of nature the Fin has added to the Norwegian character. The Fin admixture has been a great and essential factor in the composition of the mental qualities of our people at the present day.

I have often talked with people about this Finnish admixture, which, in a near degree, is looked upon almost as a disgrace, and I have found a surprisingly large number who were secretly of my opinion. Finnish admixture makes energetic, logical, bold, enterprising men; it has, to a great extent, given a backbone to the character of our Eastland and Trondhjem people. In Nordland, on the contrary, the Lap element is predominant, and has in a measure altered the character of the people. The Fin-Norwegian is master of Nordland nature; the Lap-Norwegian is subject to it, and suffers under its oppression.

Nature's contrasts in Nordland are too great and extreme for the mind of the race that lives there not to be exceedingly liable to receive permanent injury from them. The extreme melancholy and sadness which is found there in the poor man, and which so often results in mental derangement and suicide, has most undoubtedly its connection with and reason in these natural conditions; in the long winter darkness with its oppressive, overwhelming scenes that crush down the mind in light-forsaken loneliness; and in the strong and sudden impressions that, in the dark season as well as in the light, affect all too violently the delicate inner fibers of being. I have thought over these things as perhaps no one else has done – thought, while I myself have been suffering under them; and I understand – although again, when it is a question of my own person, I do not understand it in the least – why "second sight," *fremsynethed* as it is called in Nordland, can there, just as in the Shetland and Orkney Isles, make its appearance, and be inherited in a family. I understand that it is a disease of the mind, which no treatment, no intelligence or reflection can cure. A visionary is born with an additional sense of sight. Beside his two sound eyes, he has the power of looking into a world that others have only a suspicion of, and when the occasion comes it is his doom to be obliged to use his extraordinary power; it will not be stopped with books or by intelligent reflection; it will not be suppressed even here in the "enlightened capital": it can at the most only be darkened for a while with the curtain of forgetfulness.

Ah! when I think how, at home in Nordland, I pictured to myself the king's palace in Kristiania, with pinnacles and towers standing out grandly over the town, and the king's men like a golden stream from the castle court right up to the throne-room; or Akershus fortress, when the thundering cannon announce the king's arrival, and the air is filled with martial music and mighty royal commands; when I think how I pictured to myself "the high hall of light," the University, as a great white chalk mountain, always with the sunshine on its windowpanes; or how I imagined the Storthing* Hall, and the men who frequent it, whose names, magnified by fancy, echoed up to us, as though for each one there rang through the air a mighty resounding bell, names like Foss, Sörenssen, Jonas Anton Hjelm, Schweigaard, and many others; when I compare what I, up in the north, imagined about all this, with the "for our small conditions – most respectable reality," in which I now live and move – it is like a card-castle of illusions, as high as Snehætten,† falling over me. Until I was over twenty years of age, I lived only in a northern fairyland, and I am now for the first time born into the world of reality: I have been spellbound in my own fancy.

If I were to tell anyone all this, he would certainly – and the more sensible the man was the more surely – be of opinion that my good *Examen Artium*‡ must clearly have come about by some mistake. But if life depends on theoretical reasoning and knowledge, I have, thank God, as good abilities as most men. And I know that in them I have a pair of pliant oars, with which, as long as I require to do so, I shall be able to row my boat through practical life without running aground. The load which I have in the boat, at times so very heavy, but then again so blissfully beautiful, no one shall see.

I feel a longing to weep away the whole of this northern fairy tale of mine, and would do it if I could only weep away my life with it. But why wish to lose all the loveliness, all the illusion, when I must still bear with me to my dying day the sadness it has laid upon me?

It will be a relief to me in quiet hours to put down my recollections of this home of mine, which so few down here understand. It is the tale of a poor mentally-diseased man, and in it there are more of his own impressions than of outward events.

---

* Norwegian parliament

† Snehætten – a mountain in the Dovre range, 7400 feet high.

‡ *Artium* – an examination to be passed before admittance to the University is granted.

# PART III

# *Chapter I*
## HOME

My father was a country merchant, and owned the trading-place, ——ven in West Lofoten. He was really from Trondhjem, whence he had come north, as a destitute boy, in one of those small vessels which are sent from that city to Lofoten, to trade during the fishing season. In his youth he had gone through a great deal, and had even worked for a time in a boat's crew, as a simple fisherman, until he at last got a place as shop-boy with Erlandsen the merchant, whose son-in-law he became.

My father, in middle age, was a handsome man, black-haired and dark-skinned, with sharp, energetic features, and in height rather short than tall. He always wore a brown duffel, seaman's jacket, and glazed hat. In manner he was stern, and not very accessible; it was said, too, that he was rather a hard man – for which the severe school of life through which he had passed was perhaps to blame. If this manner, on the one hand, made him few friends, on the other, it gained for him a greater confidence in business matters, in which he was prompt and expeditious, always claiming to the utmost what he considered to be his due. People feared him, and would not willingly be on bad terms with him.

We have generally only flashing recollections of what has happened before our eighth year, but these flashes last for a whole lifetime. I have in my mind just such a picture of my poor unhappy mother. I know her better from that than from all I have heard about her since; from what I have been told she must have had fair hair and soft blue eyes, have been pale and delicate, and in figure rather tall. She was also very quiet and melancholy.

She was Erlandsen's only daughter, and was married to my father while he was yet a subordinate in Erlandsen's service, and it was said that it was the old man who brought about the union, thinking it the best way to provide for her future.

I remember a warm summer day, and the mowers in their shirt-sleeves, mowing with long scythes, out in the meadow: I was with my mother, as she passed by them, knitting. Outside the fence lay a half-bare rocky hill, behind which my mother had a bench. Above this on a stony heap grew raspberry bushes, and beside them stood a few small birch trees. While I was scrambling about among the stones, picking raspberries, father called my mother.

When she had gone away, there came over to me from the other side of the hill a tall, pale lady, who seemed older than mother, dressed in black, with a stand-up, white, frilled collar; she looked at me very kindly, and stretched out to me a wild rose spray she had in her hand.

I did not feel at all afraid, and it did not seem as if she were a stranger. Then she nodded sadly to me in farewell, and went back the same way she had come.

When mother returned I told her that such a kind, strange lady had been there, but she must have been in great sorrow, and now she was gone.

My mother – I remember it, as if it were yesterday – stood still for a minute, as white as a sheet, looking at me with anguish in her eyes, as if we were both going to die, then she threw her arms above her head, and fell fainting to the ground.

I was too frightened to cry, but I remember that, while she lay stretched insensible on the grass by the bench, I threw myself upon her, crying, "Mother! mother!"

A little while after I had come running to father, who stood in his shirt-sleeves over in the meadow, mowing with the others, and had said, sobbing, that mother was dead.

From that hour my mother was out of her mind. For many years she had to be constantly watched in her own room, and my father must have had many a sad hour. Afterwards she was taken to a lunatic asylum in Trondhjem, where two years later she died, without having come to her right mind for one moment.

The person who had the charge of me during this time was old Anne Kvæn, a pock-marked, masculine-looking woman, with little brown eyes, rough, iron-grey hair, strongly marked, almost witchlike features, and as a rule a short, black clay pipe in her mouth. She had been my mother's nurse, and was attached to her with her whole soul. When my mother went out of her mind, she begged earnestly to become her guardian in the blue room; but this had to be given up, as it was evident that it was just her presence that most excited the patient's mind. My mother could not bear to see father either, and me they never dared show her at all.

Old Anne Kvæn had been my mother's only confidante. She was extremely superstitious and strange. In her imagination, hobgoblins and gnomes occupied the store-house and boat-house, as surely as my father resided in the main building; and under the mountain to the east of the harbor, the underground people carried on, invisibly, their fishing and trading with Bergen, just as my father did his, visibly, in the world. Old Anne had certainly filled my poor mother's head with her mystic superstition, to no less an extent than she did mine. There were all kinds of marks and signs to be made from morning till night, and she always wore an uneasy look, as though she were keeping watch. When a boat came in, you ought to turn towards the sea, and spit, and mutter a few words against sea-sprites. She could see every man's double.* On its account the door must be shut to quickly after anyone had gone out; and she could always hear a warning beforehand when father was coming home from a journey.

When Anne Kvæn had no longer leave to go into the blue room to my mother, she silently went through all kinds of performances outside the door. I remember once standing on the stairs, and seeing her bowing and curtseying, wetting her finger every now and then, drawing on the door with it, and muttering, until I fled in terror.

In her incantation formulæ, the word "Jumala" often occurred, the name of the Bjarmers' old god, whose memory, in the far north, is not so completely eradicated as one would think, and who to this day has perhaps some sacrificial stone or other on the wide mountain wastes of Finland. Against Lap witchcraft – and a suspicion of it was fastened on almost every Lap boat that landed at the quay – she also had her charms; she apparently melted down Fin and Christian gods together in her mystical incantations, for the confounding of Lap witchcraft.

In the midst of such mental impressions as these, I grew up.

The parsonage, with the white-towered church beside it, lay only a short way from us, down by the sea, on the right-hand side of the bay, looking out from our trading-place, which lay farther in.

There was a tutor in the place – we always called him "the student" – and I went to lessons every day with the minister's two children, a bright boy of the name of Carl, who was a year younger than I, namely twelve, and his sister Susanna, of exactly the same age as myself, a blue-eyed wild child, with a quantity of yellow hair, which was always requiring to be pushed back from her forehead; when she could do so

* The spirit which everyone is supposed to have as a follower and companion through life.

unnoticed by the student, she made all kinds of faces and grimaces across at us, to make us laugh.

The tutor was, in fact, exceedingly strict, and inspired the greatest respect. The torture in which we sat when at school, not daring to look up at one another for fear our laughter should break out, was really anything but pleasant; for every time it exploded we fared very badly; in the first place, we had our hair pulled and our ears boxed, and in the next, long written harangues in our mark-books about our behavior.

Susanna was often utterly merciless; it came to such a pass, that with only a little wink in the corner of her eye, she could instantly put us in a state of fever, so that we would sit with cheeks as red as apples, and our eyes fastened on our books, until we could contain ourselves no longer. She tried especially to work upon me, though she knew I must pay dearly for misconduct at home; for father was a severe man, who had very little comprehension of children.

In play hours, we romped with more animation than children generally indulge in.

In contrast to the strict, gloomy life at home, with father always either out on business, or up in the office; where, from the blue room, often came noises and cries from my poor insane mother, and where Anne Kvæn was always going about, like a wandering spirit, playing with the parsonage children was like a life in some other and happier, more sunshiny part of the globe.

# Chapter II

## ON THE SHORE

The shore is an even more attractive playground for children in Nordland than here in the south of Norway. At low-tide there is a much longer stretch of beach than here.

The sandy bottom lies bare, with pools in it here and there, in which small fish swim, while down by the sea there sits a solitary gull on a stone, or a sea-fowl walks by the water's edge. The fine, wave-marked sand is full of heaps, covered with lines, left by the large, much sought after bait-worms, that burrow down into the earth. Hidden among the stones, or in the masses of seaweed, lie the quick, transparent, shrimplike sand-hoppers, which dart through the shallow water when they are pursued. They are used by small boys as bait, upon a bent pin, to catch young coal-fish.

Upon the high grassy hill above the beach, among some large stones, we three children built our own warehouse of flat stone slabs, with store-house, boat-house and quay below.

In the boat-house we had all kinds of boats, small and great, from the four-oared punt up to the ten-oared galley, some of wood and bark, others of the boat-shaped, blue mussel shells. Our greatest pride, the large yacht – a great, mended trough, with one mast and a deck, that was constantly being fitted out for the Bergen market – was still not the best; and I can remember how I many a time sat in church and made believe that we owned the splendid, full-rigged ship, with cannon, that hung under the chancel arch,* and how, while the minister was preaching, I pictured to myself all kinds of sailing-tours, which Carl and Susanna, but especially Susanna, should look on at in wonder. That ship was the only thing that was wanting to my happiness.

In the bay, by father's quay, there was a deep, shelving bank, where,

* A ship, symbolical of the church, often hangs in Norwegian churches.

at the end of the summer, came shoals of young cod-fish and other small fry; and there we boys carried on our fishing, each with his linen thread and bent pin. We cut the fish open, and hung them over the drying poles standing in the field over by our own warehouse for the preparation of dried fish, and we let the liver stand in small tubs to rot until it became train-oil. Both products were then duly put away in our store house, ready "to go to Bergen" later on, in the yacht; and Heaven knows we worked and slaved as eagerly and earnestly at our work as the grown-up people did at theirs, yet the only real return we had for it was the sunshine we got over our sunburned, happy faces.

Carl was a slenderly-built boy, who generally followed his more energetic sister in everything. Both children had thick yellow hair; Susanna's curled in ringlets that seemed to twinkle round her head every time she moved – which, as already said, she constantly did with a toss of her head, to keep her hair off her forehead. Both had alike a fair, brilliant complexion, and beautiful blue eyes. I do not know whether Susanna at that time was tall or short for her age – I only know I thought her at least of the same height as myself, though she must really have been half a head shorter; the difference was probably made up by my admiration.

I remember her, as she went to church on Sundays with her mother, a little, pale, soberly-clad, busy woman, who was always, except on Sunday mornings, knitting a long, dreary stocking. Susanna walked along the sand-strewn path to church in a white or blue dress, with a dark shepherdess hat on her head, a little white pocket-handkerchief folded behind a very large old hymn-book, and white stockings, and shoes with a band crossed over the instep. I did not think there could be a prettier costume in the world than Susanna's Sunday dress.

In church the minister's family sat in the first pew, right under the pulpit, and we – my father and I – a few pews behind; and we children exchanged many a Freemason's sign, intelligible only to ourselves.

But once Susanna wounded me deeply, even to bitter tears. It became evident to me that she had made my father the subject of one of her lively remarks. With his good strong voice, he used to sing the hymns in the simple country fashion, very loud; but – what I and many others considered very effective – at the end of each verse he added a peculiar turn to the last note, which did not belong to the tune, and was of his own composition. This had been made a subject of remark at the parsonage, and, like a little pitcher, Susanna had ears. When she noticed that I had found this out, she looked very unhappy.

When Carl was thirteen, he was sent to the grammar-school in Bergen, and the "expensive" tutor went away by the last steamboat that same autumn.

From this time Susanna's education was carried on by her parents, and I was obliged to acquire my learning from the clerk, a good-natured old man, who himself knew very little more than how to play the violin, which he did with passion, and a sympathetic if uncultivated taste.

When the clerk had gained my father's permission for me to learn the violin – and I, like him, preferred this kind of entertainment to learning lessons – three whole years, in other words, the time until I was sixteen years of age, were divided between violin-playing and idleness.

Perhaps if my mind, during this period of my life, had been properly kept under the daily discipline of work, much in me might have been developed differently. At it was, the whole of my imaginary life was unfortunately put into my own power, and I laid the foundation of fancies which afterwards gained the mastery over my life, to a ruinous extent. Some strongly impressionable natures require that the dividing line drawn in everyone's consciousness between fancy and reality, shall be constantly and thoroughly maintained, lest it be obliterated at certain points, and the real and the imaginary become confused.

Although we no longer had the same abundant opportunities for meeting as before, Susanna and I were, notwithstanding, constant and confidential playmates throughout our childhood.

When she had anything to confide to me, she generally watched by the gate that crossed the road by the parsonage lands, at the time when I went to or came from the clerk's.

One day, as I came homewards along the road, with my books under my arm, she was sitting in her blue-checked frock and straw hat, on the steps by the side of the gate. She looked as if she were in a very bad temper, and I could see at once that I was in for something.

She did not answer my greeting; but when I attempted to slip through the gate a little more quickly than she liked, she asked me in an irritated tone if it were true, as they said, that I was so lazy that they could make nothing of me at home.

Susanna had often teased me; but what wounded me this time was that I saw that they had been making my father and me the subject of censorious remarks at the parsonage, and that Susanna had been a party to it. Had I known that she now sat there as my defeated advocate, I should certainly have done otherwise than I did, for with an offended look I passed on without bestowing a word upon her.

When I came home, I heard that the minister and my father had had a disagreement in the Court of Reconciliation. The minister, who was a commissioner of that court, had said that he thought my father went too quickly forward in a certain case, and my father had given him a hasty answer. It was on this occasion that judgment was passed upon us in the parsonage.

This state of affairs between our elders caused some shyness between us children, and I remember that at first I was even afraid to go by the parsonage, for fear of meeting the minister on the road.

Susanna, however, made several attempts at advances; but at the first glimpse of her blue-checked frock I always went a long way round, through the field above the road, or waited among the trees until she was gone.

For some time I saw nothing of her; but one day, as I was going through the gate, I saw written in pencil on the white board of the post that marked the rode*: "You are angry with me, but S. is not at all angry with you."

I knew the large clumsy writing well, and I went back to the gate two or three times that day to read it over and over again. It was Susanna in a new character; I saw her in thought behind the letters as behind a balustrade. In the afternoon I wrote underneath: "Look on the back of the post!" and there I wrote: "D. is not angry with S. either."

The next day Susanna was standing by the fence in the garden when I passed, but pretended not to see me; she probably repented having been so ready to make advances.

Although outwardly their relations were polite in the extreme, in reality my father's intercourse with the minister was from this time broken off; they never, except on special occasions and in response to a solemn invitation, set foot within one another's door. This again gave a kind of clandestine character to the intercourse between me and Susanna. No command was laid upon us, yet we only met, as it were, by stealth.

We were both lonely children. Susanna sat at home, a prisoner to everyday tediousness, under her mother's watchful eye, and in my dreary home I always had a feeling of cold and fright, and as if all gladness were over with Susanna at the parsonage. It was therefore not surprising that we were always longing to be together.

As we grew older, opportunities were less frequent, but the longing only became the greater by being repressed, and the moments we could spend together gradually acquired, unknown to us, another than the old childish character. To talk to her had now become a solace to me, and many a day I haunted the parsonage lands, only to get a glimpse of her.

* Rode – a length of road. The high-road is divided into rodes, and the division between these is marked by posts, on which stand the names of the houses, whose owners have to keep that portion of the road in repair.

I was about sixteen, when one morning, as I passed the parsonage garden, she beckoned to me, and handed me a flower over the wall, and then she hastily ran in, right across the carrot beds, as if she were afraid someone would see.

It was the first time it had struck me how beautiful she was, and for many a day I thought of her as she stood there in the garden among the bushes with the morning sun shining down upon her.

# Chapter III

## THE SERVANTS' HALL

The ghostly spirit which ran through our house, first had free outlet down in the servants' hall, when the men and maids, and the wayfarers who were putting up for the night, sat in the evening in the red glow from the stove, and told all kinds of tales about shipwrecks and ghosts.

On the bench in the space between the stove and the wall, sat the strong, handsome man Jens with his carpentering and repairs; he used to do his work, and listen in silence to the others. By the stove "Komag-Nils" busied himself with greasing komags* or skins – he had this name, because he made komags. Komag-Nils was a little fellow, with untidy yellow hair, which hung over his eyes, and a face as round as a moon, on which the nose looked like a little button; when he laughed, his wide thin-lipped mouth and large jaws gave him almost the expression of a death's-head. His small, watery eyes blinked at you mysteriously, but showed plainly that he was not wanting in common sense. It was he, in fact, who could tell the greatest number of stories, but still more was it he who could get a stranger to tell stories of the visible or the invisible world just as they occurred to him.

A third man went by a nickname, which, however, they never gave him within his hearing; Anders Lead-head, was so called, because he now and then had bad fits of drinking, and nearly lost his place in consequence. And yet in his way he was extremely capable. In any real dilemma – in a storm – he rose at once to the responsible post of captain in the boat; for there was but one opinion of his capability as a sailor. When the danger was over, he fell back again into the insignificant man.

A girl of twenty years of age, whom we called French Martina, was also one of the regular servants of the house. She seemed of a totally different race of beings from the ordinary Nordlander, was quick and

* Komag – a peculiar kind of leather boot used by the Fins.

lively, with thick, curly black hair, round a brown oval face with strikingly regular features. She was slenderly built, of middle height, and had a good figure. Her eyes, beneath strongly marked, black eyebrows, were as black as coal; and when she was angry, they could flash fire. She was in love with the silent Jens, and was extremely jealous, without the slightest cause. It was said that these two would make a match when he had been on two or three more fishing expeditions, but the matter was not officially announced at any rate, I think because Jens made a passive resistance as long as he could, and never actually proposed to her. French Martina was, by birth, one of the illegitimate children of those fishing districts, whose fathers are foreign skippers or sailors. Her father was said to have been a French sailor.

I was strictly forbidden by my father to go into the servants' hall in the evening; he knew very well that a good many things were said there that were not fit for children's ears. But then, on the other hand, it was just down there that the most interesting things in the world were talked about. The consequence was that I used to steal down secretly. I remember how, one dark autumn evening, when I had slipped in, I listened, while Komag-Nils – the man with the yellow hair and death's-head grin when he laughed – told a dreadful ghost story from Erlandsen's predecessor's time.

At that time there stood an old store-house not far from the parsonage. One Christmas Eve they sat drinking and merry-making in the warehouse. At eleven o'clock the ale gave out, and a man named Rasmus, who was a strong, courageous fellow, was sent to the store-house, where the beer-cask lay, to fill a large pewter jug, which he took with him. When he got there, Rasmus set the lantern on the cask, and began to draw. When the jug was full, and he was just meditating putting it to his lips, he saw, over the beer barrel, lying with its body in the shadow, where all the barrels stood in a row, a terribly big, broad, dark form, from which there came an icy breath, as if from a door that stood open; it blinked at him with two great eyes like dull, horn lanterns, and said: "A thief at the Christmas ale!" But Rasmus did not neglect his opportunity. He flung the heavy jug right in the goblin's face, and ran away as fast as his legs would carry him. Outside there was moonlight on the snow; he heard cries and howls down on the shore, and became aware that goblins were pursuing him in ever-increasing numbers. When he came to the churchyard wall they were close upon him, and in his extremity he bethought himself of shouting over the wall: "Help me now, all ye dead!" for the dead are enemies of the goblins. He heard them all rising, and noises and yells as of a battle followed. He himself was closely pursued by a goblin, who was just on the point of springing upon him as he seized the latch of the door, and got safely in. But then he fell fainting on the floor. The next day – the first Christmas Day* – the people going to church saw, strewn all around on the graves, pieces of coffin-boards, and all kinds of old sodden oars, and such timbers as usually sink to the bottom after a shipwreck. They were the weapons that the dead and the goblins had used, and from various things it could be gathered that the dead were the victors. They also found both the pewter jug and the lantern down in the store-house. The pewter jug had been beaten flat against the goblin's skull, and the goblin had smashed the lantern when Rasmus escaped.

Komag-Nils could also tell a great deal about people with second sight and their visions of things, sometimes in the spirit world, sometimes in actual life, of which they either feel a warning, or – as if in a kind of atmospheric reflection before their mental vision – can see what is happening at that very moment in far distant places. They may be sitting in merry company, and all at once, becoming pale and disturbed, they gaze absently before them into space. They see all kinds of things, and sometimes an exclamation escapes them, such as: "A fire has broken out in Merchant N.N.'s buildings in ——vaagen!" or "Trondhjem is burning now!" Sometimes they see a long funeral procession passing, with such distinctness that they can describe the place and appearance of every man in it, the coffin and the streets through which the procession wends its way. They will say: "A great man is being buried down in Kristiania"; and when the news comes, it always corresponds with their statement. It may happen, at sea, that such a man will say to the captain that he will do well to go out of his course for a little while; and he is always obeyed, for the crew are quite sure that he beholds in front of the ship what none of them perceive, perhaps a goblin in his half-boat, or a specter, or something else that brings misfortune.

One of Komag-Nils' many stories of this kind had happened to an acquaintance of his during the winter fishing. The weather had been very stormy for two days, but on the third had so far lulled that one of the boats' crews that had been lodging in the fishing hut, thought that it would be quite possible to draw their nets. But the rest did not care to venture. Now it is a custom that the different boats' crews shall give each other a hand in launching the boats, and this was now to be done. When they came down to the ten-oared boat, which was drawn a good way up the beach, they found both oars and thwarts reversed, and, in addition to this, it was impossible, even with their united efforts, to

* In Norway, Christmas Day is called "first Christmas Day"; the day after, "second Christmas Day," and so on to the end of the week.

move it. They tried once, twice, three times without avail. And then one of them, who was known to have second sight, said that from what he saw, it was better that they should not touch the boat that day: it was too heavy for human power. In one of the crews that put up in the fishing-hut there was a lively boy of fourteen, who entertained them the whole time with tricks of all kinds, and was never quiet. He took up a huge stone and threw it with all his might into the stern of the boat. Instantly there rushed out, visible to everyone, a gnome in seaman's dress with a great bunch of seaweed for a head. It had been sitting at the stern weighing down the boat, and now rushed out into the sea, dashing the water up in spray round it as it went. After that the boat went smoothly into the water. The man with the second sight looked at the boy, and said he ought not to have done as he had; but the boy only laughed and said that he did not believe in goblins or spirits. In the night, when they had come home and lay sleeping in the hut, at about twelve o'clock they heard the boy crying for help. One of the men thought, too, he saw by the dim light of the oil lamp a great hand stretching in from the door up to the bench on which the boy lay. Before they had so far collected themselves as to lay hold of the hand, the boy, crying out and resisting, was already dragged to the door. And now a hard struggle took place in the doorway, the goblin pulling the boy by the legs, while the whole crew held him by the arms and the upper part of his body. In this way, at the hour of midnight, he was dragged backwards and forwards in the half-open doorway, now the men, now the goblin, having the better of the struggle. All at once the goblin let go his hold, so that the whole crew fell over one another backwards on to the floor. But the boy was dead, and they understood that it was only then that the goblin had let go. The following winter they used to hear wailings at midnight in the fishing-hut, and they had no peace until it was moved away to another spot.

The Nordlander has the same, or even a greater pride in owning the fastest sailing-boat, that the East countryman in many places has in having the fastest trotting-horse. A really good boat is talked of in as many districts in the north, as, a really fine trotter would be in the south. All sorts of traditions about the speed and wonderful racing powers of the boats are current in Nordland, and romantic tales are told of some of them. The best boats in Nordland now came from Ranen, where boat building has made great strides. To build a good boat with the correct water-lines requires genius, and cannot be learned theoretically; for it is a matter of special skill on the part of the builder of each boat. Ill-constructed boats are sometimes put together but they are, of course, unsatisfactory and sail only moderately well. The Nordland boat-builders have long since discovered the high fore and aft, sharp-keeled boat, to be the most practical, with one mast and a broad, prettily cut square sail admirably suited to what is most required, rapid sailing in fore and side winds, though less so for tacking. The boat is exactly the same shape under water as the fast-sailing clippers for which the English and Americans have of late become famed. What it has cost the Nordlanders to perfect the form that now enables them almost to fly before the wind, away from mighty curling billows which would bury the boat, if they reached it; how many generations have suffered and toiled and thought over, and corrected this shape under pain of death, so to speak, for every mistake made! In short, the history of the Nordland boat, from the days of men who first waged war with the ocean up there, to this day is a forgotten Nordland saga, full of the great achievements of the steadily toiling workman.

One winter's evening in January, a little while before the fishing began, I heard a story told by a man of one of the large boats' crews who were then spending the night at our house. He was started by two or three of Komag-Nils' stories, and wanted to show us that where he came from, down at Dönö near Ranen, in Helgeland, there were as many and as wonderful stories and boats, as with us in Nordland. The narrator was a little, quick-speaking fellow, who sat the whole time rocking backwards and forwards, and fidgeting upon the bench, while he talked. With his sharp nose, and round, reddish little eyes, he resembled a restless sea-bird on a rock. Every now and then he broke off to dive down into his provision box, as if every time he did so he took out of it a fresh piece of his story. The story was as follows:

On Kvalholmen, in Helgeland, there lived a poor fisherman named Elias, with his wife Karen, who had formerly been servant at the minister's over at Alstadhaug. They had put up a cottage at Kvalholmen, and Elias was now in the Lofoten fishing-trade, working for daily wages.

It was pretty evident that lonely Kvalholmen was haunted. When the husband was away, the wife heard many dismal noises and cries, which could not come from anything good. One day when she was up on the mountain, cutting grass for winter fodder for the two or three sheep they owned, she distinctly heard the sound of talking on the beach below, but dared not look to see who was there.

Every year there came a child, but the parents were both industrious. When seven years had passed there were six children in the cottage; and that same autumn the man had scraped together so much that he thought he could afford to buy a six-oared boat, and henceforward sail to the fishing in his own boat.

One day as he was walking along with a halibut pike[*] in his hand, meditating over his intention, he stumbled unexpectedly, upon an immense seal, which lay sunning itself behind a rock down on the shore. The seal was quite as little prepared for the man as the man for it. Elias, however, was not slow; from the rock where he stood he thrust the long heavy pike into its back, just below the head.

And then there was a scene! All at once the seal raised itself upon its tail straight up in the air, as high as a boat-mast, showed its teeth and looked at Elias with two bloodshot eyes, so maliciously and venomously, that he was nearly frightened out of his senses. Then the seal rushed straight into the sea, leaving a track of blood-tinged foam behind it. Elias saw nothing more of it; but the same afternoon the halibut pike, with the iron point broken off, was washed up at the landing-stage in Kval creek where the house stood.

Elias thought no more of the affair. The same autumn he bought his six-oared boat, for which he had put up a little boat-house during the summer.

One night as he lay thinking about this new boat of his, it struck him that in order to make it thoroughly secure he ought, perhaps, to put one more plank to support it on each side. He was so fond of the boat, that it was nothing but a pleasure for him to get up and go with a lantern to look at it.

While he stood holding the light up over the boat, he suddenly caught sight of a face in the corner, upon a heap of fishing-net, that exactly resembled the seal's. The creature showed its teeth angrily at him and the light, its mouth seeming the whole time to grow wider and wider, and then a huge man rushed out through the boat-house door, but not too quickly for Elias to see, by the light of the lantern, that out of his back there stuck a long iron spike. Now Elias began to understand a little; but still he was more afraid on account of his boat than for his own life, and he sat in the boat himself, with the lantern, and kept guard. When his wife came to look for him in the morning she found him sleeping, with the extinguished lantern by his side.

One morning in the following January when he put out to fish with two men in his boat besides himself, he heard in the dark a voice that came from a rock at the entrance to the creek. It laughed scornfully, and said: "When you get a ten-oared boat, take care, Elias!"

However, it was many years before anything happened to the ten-oared boat, and by that time his eldest son, Bernt, was seventeen. That

---

* A long wooden pole with a barbed iron point to spear halibut with.

autumn Elias went into Ranen with his whole family in the six-oared boat, to exchange it for a ten-oared boat. Only a newly confirmed Fin girl, whom they had taken in some years before, was left at home.

Elias had in his eye a half-decked ten-oared boat, which the best boat-builder in Ranen had finished and tarred that very autumn. Elias knew very well what a boat should be, and thought he had never seen one so well built under the water-line. Above, on the contrary, it was only fairly good, so that to anyone less experienced it looked heavy, and with no beauty to speak of.

The builder knew this just as well as Elias. He said he believed it would be the first boat in Ranen for sailing; but that, all the same, Elias should have it cheap, if he would only promise one thing, and that was, not to make any alteration in it, not so much as to put a line on the tar. Only when Elias had expressly promised this did he get the boat.

But "the fellow," who had taught the builder the shape for his boats below water-line – above it, he was obliged to work as he could by himself, and that was often poorly enough – had probably advised him beforehand, to sell it cheaply, so that Elias should have it, and also to make it a condition that the boat should not be marked in any way. The cross[*] usually painted fore and aft, did not, therefore, appear on the boat.

Elias now thought of sailing home, but first went to the shop and laid in a supply of Christmas goods including a little keg of brandy for himself and his family. Delighted as he was with his purchase, both he and his wife took that day a little more than was good for them, and Bernt, the son, also had a taste.

Their shopping done, they set out to sail the new boat home. It had no other ballast than himself, his wife and children, and the Christmas fare. His son Bernt sat in the fore-part, his wife, with the help of the second son, held the halyard, and Elias sat at the helm, while the two younger boys, twelve and fourteen years of age, were to take turns at baling.

They had eight miles[†] to sail, and when they got out to sea, it was pretty evident that they would come to prove the boat the first time she was used. A storm was gradually rising, and the foam-crests began to break on the great waves.

Now Elias saw what sort of a boat he had; she cleared the waves like a sea-bird, without so much as a drop coming in, and he therefore judged that he did not need to take in a reef, which in an ordinary ten-oared

---

* Customary with fishermen in Nordland to keep evil spirits away.

† About thirty-eight English miles = eight Norwegian sea miles.

boat he would be obliged to do in such weather.

Later in the day he noticed, not far off on the sea, another ten-oared boat fully manned and with four reefs in the sail, exactly as he had. Her course was the same as his, and he thought it rather strange that he had not seen her before. She seemed desirous of racing with him, and when Elias saw this he could not refrain from letting out another reef.

The boat now flew with the speed of an arrow past naze, island and rock, till Elias thought he had never been for such a splendid sail before, and the boat now showed herself to be, as she really was, the first boat in Ranen.

In the meantime the sea had grown rougher, and two considerable waves had already broken over them. They broke in at the bow where Bernt sat, and flowed out to leeward near the stern.

Since it had become darker, the other boat had kept quite close, and they were now so near to one another that a scoop could have been thrown across from one boat to the other.

And thus they sailed, side by side, in the growing storm, throughout the evening. The fourth reef of the sail ought properly to have been taken in, but Elias was loath to give up the race, and he thought he would wait until they took a reef in over in the other boat, where it must be needed quite as much as in his. The brandy keg went round from time to time, for there was now both cold and wet to be kept out.

The phosphorescence that played in the black waves near Elias's boat shone weirdly in the foam round the other boat, which seemed to plow up and roll waves of fire about her sides. By their bright light he could even distinguish the spars and ropes in her. He could also distinctly see the men on board, with sou'westers on their heads; but as their windward side was nearest, they all had their backs turned to him, and were nearly hidden by the gunwale.

Suddenly there broke over the bows, where Bernt sat, a tremendous wave whose white crest Elias had long seen through the darkness. It seemed to stop the whole boat for an instant, the timbers quivered and shook under its weight, and when the boat, which for a few seconds lay half-capsized, righted herself and went on her way again, it streamed out astern. While this was happening, he fancied there were ghastly cries in the other boat. But when it was over, his wife, who sat at the halyard, said in a voice that cut him to the heart: "Good God! Elias, that wave took Martha and Nils with it!" – these were their youngest children, the former nine, the latter seven years old, who had been sitting in the bow, near Bernt. To this Elias only answered: "Don't let go the rope, Karen, or you will lose more!"

It was now necessary to take in the fourth reef, and, when that was done, Elias found that the fifth ought to be taken in too, for the storm was increasing; yet in order to sail the boat free of the ever-increasing seas he dared not, on the other hand, take in more sail than was absolutely necessary. But the little sail they could carry became gradually less and less. The spray dashed in their faces, and Bernt and his next youngest brother Anton, who till now had helped his mother with the halyard, were at last obliged to hold the yard, an expedient resorted to when the boat cannot even bear to go with the last reef – in this case the fifth.

The companion boat, which had in the meantime vanished, now suddenly appeared again beside them with exactly the same amount of sail as Elias's boat; and he began rather to dislike the look of the crew on board of her. The two men who stood there holding the yard, whose pale faces he could distinguish under the sou'westers, seemed to him, in the curious light from the breaking foam, more like corpses than living beings, and apparently they did not speak a word.

A little to windward he saw once more the high white crest of another huge wave coming through the dark, and he prepared for it in time. The boat was laid with her stem in a slanting direction to it, and with as much sail as she could carry, in order to give her sufficient speed to cleave it and sail right through it. In it rushed with the roar of a waterfall; again the boat half heeled over, and when the wave was past his wife no longer sat at the halyard, and Anton no longer stood holding the yard – they had both gone overboard.

This time, too, Elias thought he heard the same horrible cries in the air; but in the midst of them he distinctly heard his wife calling his name in terror. When he comprehended that she was washed overboard, he only said: "In Jesus' name!" and then was silent. His inclination was to follow her, but he felt, too, that he must do what he could to save the rest of the freight he had on board – namely, Bernt and his two other sons, the one twelve, the other fourteen, who had baled the boat for a time, but had now found a place in the stern behind their father.

Bernt now had to mind the sail alone; and he and his father, as far as was possible, helped one another. Elias dared not let go the tiller, and he held it firmly with a hand of iron that had long lost feeling from the strain.

After a while the companion boat appeared again; as before, it had been absent for a time. Now, too, Elias saw more of the big man who sat in the stern in the same place as himself. Out of his back, below the sou'wester, when he turned, stuck a six-inch-long iron spike which Elias thought he ought to know. And now, in his own mind, he had come to a clear understanding upon two points: one was that it was no other than the sea-goblin himself who was steering his half-boat by his side and was leading him to destruction, and the other, that it was so ordained that he was sailing his last voyage that night. For he who sees the goblin on the sea is a lost man. He said nothing to the others for fear of making them lose courage; but he silently committed his soul to God.

For the last few hours he had been obliged to go out of his course for the storm; the air too became thick with snow, and he saw that he would have to wait for dawn before he could find out his whereabouts. In the meantime they sailed on. Now and then the boys in the stern complained of the cold, but there was nothing to be done in the wet, and moreover Elias's thoughts were of very different things. He had such an intense desire for revenge, that, if he had not had the lives of his three remaining children to defend, he would have attempted by a sudden turn of his own boat to run into and sink the other, which still, as if in mockery, kept by his side, and whose evil object he understood only too well. If the halibut pike could wound the goblin before, then surely a knife or a landing-hook might now, and he felt that he would gladly give his life for a good blow at the monster who had so unmercifully taken his dearest from him, and still wanted more victims.

Between three and four in the morning Elias saw, advancing through the dark, another foam-crest, so high that at first he thought they must be near breakers, close to land. But he soon saw that it really was an enormous wave. Then he fancied he distinctly heard laughter over in the other boat, and the words, "Now your boat will capsize, Elias!" Elias, who foresaw the disaster, said aloud: "In Jesus' name!" and told his sons to hold on, with all their might, to the willow bands on the rowlocks when the boat went under, and not to leave go until she rose again. He made the elder boy go forward to Bernt; he himself held the younger close to him, quietly stroking his cheek, and assured himself that he had a good hold. The boat was literally buried under the foam-drift, then gradually lifted at the bow, and went under. When she rose again, keel uppermost, Elias, Bernt, and the twelve-year-old Martin still held on to the willow bands. But the third brother was gone.

The first thing to be done now was to cut the shrouds on one side, so that the mast could float beside them, instead of greatly adding to the unsteadiness of the boat underneath; and the next to get up on to the rolling keel and knock the plug in, which would let out the air underneath, so that the boat could lie still. After great exertion they succeeded in this, and then Elias, who was the first to get on to the keel, helped the others up too.

And there they sat through the long winter night, clinging convulsively with hands and knees to the keel over which the waves washed again and again.

After two or three hours had passed, Martin whom his father had supported as well as he could the whole time, died of exhaustion, and slipped down into the sea. They had already tried calling out for help several times, but gave it up, because they saw it was of no use.

While Elias and Bernt sat alone upon the overturned boat, Elias said to his son that he was quite sure he himself would go to "be with mother," but he had strong hopes that Bernt might yet be saved, if he only held out like a man. Then he told him of the goblin he had wounded in the back with the halibut pike, and how it had revenged itself upon him, and would not give up "until they were quits."

It was about nine in the morning, when the dawn began to show grey. Then Elias handed to Bernt, who sat by his side, his silver watch with the brass chain, which he had broken in two in drawing it out from under his buttoned-up waistcoat. He still sat for a while, but, as it grew lighter, Bernt saw that his father's face was deadly pale, his hair had parted in several places as it often does when death is near, and the skin was torn from his hands by holding on to the keel. The son knew that his father could not last long, and wanted, as well as the pitching would allow, to move along and support him; but when Elias noticed this he said: "Only hold fast, Bernt! In Jesus' name, I am going to mother" and thereupon threw himself backwards off the boat.

When the sea had got its due, it became, as everyone knows who has sat long upon an upturned boat, a good deal quieter. It became easier for Bernt to hold on; and with the growing day there came more hope. The storm lulled, and when it became quite light, it seemed to him he ought to know where he was, and that he lay drifting outside his own native place, Kvalholmen.

He began once more to call for help, but hoped most in a current which he knew set in to land at a place where a naze on the island broke the force of the waves, so that there was smooth water within. He did drift nearer and nearer, and at last came so near to one rock that the mast, which was floating by the side of the boat, was lifted up and down the slope of the rock by the waves. Stiff as all his joints were with sitting and holding on, he yet succeeded by great exertion in climbing up on to the rock, where he hauled up the mast and moored the boat.

The Fin servant-maid who was alone in the house, had thought for a few hours that she heard cries of distress, and as they continued she climbed the hill to look out. There she saw Bernt upon the rock, and the boat, bottom upwards, rocking up and down against it. She immediately ran down to the boat-house, launched the old four-oared boat, and rowed it along the shore, round the island, out to him.

Bernt lay ill under her care the whole winter, and did not go fishing that year. People thought, too, after this that he was now and then a little strange.

He had a horror of the sea, and would never go on it again. He married the Fin girl and moved up to Malangen, where he bought a clearing, and is now doing well.

# *Chapter IV*

## AMONG THE VÆTTE ROCKS

It was summer. Susanna and I were now in our seventeenth year, and it was settled that we should be confirmed in the autumn.

It was this year that my father was involved in his unequal struggle with the authorities – among whom were the sheriff and the minister – as to whether our trading-place should be a permanent stopping-place for the Nordland steamer. This was a matter of vital importance to my father, and the dispute about it, which also interested the whole district, had already begun to be rather warm.

This was, in fact, not the least important object that the sheriff had in view when he came that summer on a visit to the minister, who was a very influential man.

Outwardly there was as yet no rupture between my father and the minister, and it must have been for the purpose of manifesting this publicly that during the sheriff's visit my father was invited over to the minister's two or three times.

It was thus that my father and I were one day asked to go on a sailing-trip out to the Vætte Rocks, which lay half a mile away. We were first to fish, and then to eat milk-rings$FThe thick sour cream off the pans in which milk has been set up. on land at Gunnar's Place, a house rented from the parsonage.

There was always a certain solemnity about the occasion when the minister's white house-boat with four men at the oars glided out of the bay, and a considerable number of spectators generally stood on shore to watch it. That day, father, too, stood out on the steps, with a telescope. He had excused himself from going, but with good tact had let me go.

In the cabin, which was open on account of the heat, sat the minister's wife and the sheriff's two ladies, and outside, one on each side, the minister and the sheriff, smoking their silver-mounted meerschaum pipes, and chatting comfortably: they were college-friends. Susanna and I, together with the housemaid from Trondhjem, who was adorned for the occasion, had a place in the roomy bow. The minister's wife wanted to keep that part of the boat in which she had an immense provision basket – a regular portable larder – under her own eye. The big basket and the little lady entirely occupied one bench, while the two other ladies, with their starched dresses, quite filled up the rest of the narrow cabin.

There was not a breath stirring, and the West Fjord heaved in long, smooth swells. The fjord lay like a giant at rest, sunning itself. The wonderfully clear air allowed the eye to see over the mountain ranges, almost into eternity, while an aërial reflection – an inverted mountain, with a house under it and a couple of spouting whales – built up a fairytale for us over the blue stretch of sea. Now and then we met a sea-fowl, floating on the smooth water; and in our wake gamboled a porpoise or two.

A little before midday we got in among the Vætte Rocks, and set about fishing; for first, without considering the provision basket, we had to procure our own dinner.

On the outer side of the rocks the surf broke noisily in the still day, and sent up great white jets, or retreated with a long sucking sound, as if the ocean drew deep, regular, breaths. Restless as Susanna was, she bent over the gunwale, until her hair almost dipped in her own image in the water, to look through the transparent sea at the fish, which, at a depth of fifteen or twenty fathoms, glided in and out among the seaweed over the greenish-white bottom, and crowded round the lines with which the grown-up people with their double tackle often drew up two fish at once. In her eagerness she called me stone-blind, whenever I could not see just the fish she meant. And short-sighted I was, too, but Susanna's slightest movement interested me more than any fish.

The scene was indeed enchanting. The white boat rocked over its image, as if it hung in space. Gunnar's Place, too, lay reflected in the water, with field-patches below it, and birch-clad slopes above and around it. The air, which had, later in the day, become misty with the heat, was filled with the strong scent of foliage, such as is only known in the south when it has been raining.

In less than an hour the pail was full of fish, enough for a "boiling," and we landed.

The minister's wife meantime had a table brought out on to the grass in front of the house, and on the fine damask cloth she had placed several milk-rings. She had also made *romme gröd*$FThick cream, either sweet or sour, boiled. and, as far as space would permit, had loaded the table with courses from the provision basket.

But at last the wine and good things began to confuse the sheriff's brain a little. To the intense horror of the minister's wife, he related how her husband, grey-haired and strict as he now was, had been an unusually gay fellow in his youth, and how they had played many a mad prank together.

When the sheriff found that he had made a mistake, he tried to mend matters by a serious toast, in which he expressed a hope that, for the sake of the district, the minister would be able to defeat all the machinations of his intriguing neighbor – here he was stopped in his speech by a meaning look from the minister over at me, as I sat at the end of the table – and ended with some wandering remarks, which were meant to turn off the whole thing.

I turned cold, and the perspiration stood on my forehead, and I must have been as white as a sheet. For my father's sake, I thought I must keep up appearances, but the food stuck in my throat, and I could not swallow another mouthful. I looked across at Susanna; she was crimson.

There was a short silence, during which everyone ruminated over what had passed, until the summer day's drowsiness became too overpowering, and the minister and the sheriff, who were both accustomed to take an after-dinner nap, proposed that everyone should seek a shady place and rest for an hour.

After what had passed at table I felt utterly miserable. They had allowed so offensive an opinion about my father to escape, that it was torture to me to remain any longer in their company.

A little beyond the house, the hill sloped down into a narrow valley, with birches and willows on the ridge on both sides, and among them there flowed over the flint stones a clear, twinkling little brook, in which glided a trout or two. While the others slept, I went up along the bank, and lay down to brood in solitude over my sorrow.

I do not know how long I had lain thus; but when I looked up, Susanna sat there in great agitation. She thought they had behaved badly towards me, she said, and then, as though she could not bear to see me distressed, she silently stroked the hair back from my forehead again and again.

There was a warmth in the little hand and an eloquence in her face as she struggled to keep back her tears, that my heart, so hungering after affection, could not withstand.

I do not know how it came about, but I only remember that I stood and pressed her passionately to my heart, with my cheek against hers, and begged her to love me, only a little, and I would love her without measure the whole of my life. I remember, too, that she answered "Yes," and that we both cried.

A little while after we stood hand in hand, smiling and looking at one another. A new thought had simultaneously come to us both – that now we were engaged. Susanna was the first to give it expression, and said, as she looked at me out of the depths of her faithful blue eyes, that from this time I must always remember that she was fond of me, however unkind the others were.

We heard them calling us, and – what we had never thought of doing before – Susanna hurried on by herself a little way, so that we each came back to the others alone.

It was far on into the morning of the next day, when Anne Kvæn roused me with a shake, as she had been accustomed to do since I was a child, and told me that my father had started that morning for Tromsö. He had been up to my room before he went, and when he came down again said that I lay smiling in my sleep, and "looked so happy, poor boy!"

It was very seldom that any sympathetic words came from my father, so these are imprinted on my memory.

My father himself at that time was anything but cheerful. The steamboat dispute lay heavy on his heart, and he now wanted to try, as a last resort, to have the matter thoroughly aired in the newspapers, and it was about this that he now wanted to apply personally to a solicitor at Tromsö.

These circumstances, however, did not come to my knowledge at that time.

# *Chapter V*
# CONFIRMATION

While matters were in this state between our parents, the time came for Susanna and me to be confirmed. As I was not entered until some time after the confirmation course had begun, it was arranged that, besides the class in the church every Monday, I was to read alone with the minister on Fridays.

In his abrupt way my father made me a little private speech, in which he expressed a hope that I would not disgrace him before the minister.

The lesson up in the minister's study was an entirely new mental development for me. The big, grey-haired man, with his broad, powerful face, and massive silver spectacles, generally pushed up on to his forehead above the heavy eyebrows, sat on the sofa with his big meerschaum pipe in his mouth, and expounded, while I, smart and attentive, listened in the chair on the opposite side of the table.

I became more and more convinced that the minister must be an honorable and thoroughly sincere man, but at the same time hard and severe; for he always talked about our duties, and that we must not think that pardon would be given us if we tried to escape from them. Sometimes, too, he would be in the humor for reflections which were not quite intended for me; there were all kinds of attempts to reason away doubts that might possibly arise in matters of belief, especially about miracles, which he generally wanted to explain in a natural way. He could be exceedingly clever in his comparisons, and I used then to think in this, as in much of the strong-willed expression of his face when he talked, that I recognized Susanna's nature. The small, well-shaped hands and the well-proportioned though not tall figure, she had evidently inherited from her father, as also a certain quick movement of the head when her words were to be made more impressive than usual. But Susanna had in addition a warmth and impulsiveness, almost volcanic in their nature, which struck me as foreign to the expression that lay in the minister's cold, clear, intelligent eyes.

The minister praised me for my thoughtfulness, but repeated several times, to my secret humiliation, that I had a way of furtively looking down that I must try to get rid of. He doubtless thought that I was excessively embarrassed, perhaps, too, that I suffered under the consciousness of my father's position with regard to him.

However that may be, his cold, piercing, blue or grey eyes sometimes looked at me as if they saw right through me and cut me up like an orange, right into my secret with Susanna. I felt like a traitor who was betraying his confidence, and I pictured to myself what he would think of me one day, when he came to know all, and that during his instruction on the subject of my eternal happiness I could have sat before him so false and bold. I became more and more convinced during the lessons on the Explanation,* that my relations with Susanna, as long as they were kept a secret from her parents, were wrong, and now I was going, with this deliberate sin on my conscience, coolly and with premeditation to kneel at the Lord's Table.

These scruples haunted me at home, too, and at last became a real martyrdom to me. All sin, said the Explanation, could be forgiven, except sin against the Holy Ghost.

The deeper my imagination was plunged in meditation on this mysterious crime against Heaven, which was beyond the limits of pardon and could not be forgiven, the higher rose the torturing anxiety in my mind lest the very sin that I was now calmly and deliberately about to commit, was of that kind.

My hesitation was especially on the subject of the Sacrament, which I now boldly, and with full purpose, intended to desecrate, by concealing the fact that I was deceiving the very person that would give it to me. I tried in vain to dismiss these thoughts, or at any rate to put them off, until the very last day before confirmation. My mind became every day more uneasy, and in my imagination there arose thoughts that no longer depended on my own will, and I stood dismayed before all the visions and possibilities of hell's terror.

I dared not reassure myself by trying to get Susanna to talk about my fears; for as long as she was ignorant that what was to be done was a sin, she was not to blame; and rather than involve her with myself, I would bear my burden alone. To reveal the whole thing at the last moment to the stern minister would, of course, disclose our engagement, would be an unbearable scandal for us both, and, as I thought,

---

* Of Luther's Catechism

would only result in my losing Susanna; and this I dared not risk without her consent. The whole thing was thus knotted into an impossible ring, out of which no escape seemed possible.

On the last two Mondays when I stood in the church while the minister examined us, I often looked earnestly over at Susanna. She stood there, bright, smiling and inattentive; she suspected nothing, and could give no help.

During the days immediately before the confirmation my distress rose to fever height, several times I was scarcely in my right mind, and felt dreadfully unhappy. It seemed to me at last that I was actually throwing away my eternal happiness for Susanna's sake. At night I started up from terrifying dreams, in which I saw myself kneeling at the altar with Susanna beside me – she looking so unsuspecting, so supernaturally beautiful, while the minister stood with a face of thunder, as if he knew that a soul would now be destroyed, and that, in the Communion, he was carrying out God's vengeance. Another night I awoke with a fancy that a scornful laugh came from under the bed, and with a conviction that the Evil One lurked there, curled up like a great snake. I hid myself with a beating heart under the down quilt, until I heard people moving in the yard below in the morning, and then I ventured to fly from the room.

It was Confirmation Day.

I stood at the glass that morning, before church-time, dressing myself in my new clothes, in the "blue room," the room in which my mother had been confined during the many years she was ill. I could see, through the small-paned windows, boat after boat full of nicely-dressed confirmation candidates, with their parents in holiday costume, rowing, in the bright autumn day, across the bay, and landing, some at our pier, others at the parsonage landing-place.

An impression of solemnity suddenly filled me with despair; I thought of how all these people would come into God's kingdom as easily as they were now rowing into the sunny bay this quiet Sunday morning, while I alone stood without hope of salvation. I saw all at once that in my sad, spiritually dark home, I had always, from childhood upwards, really had a feeling in my inmost heart that happiness and blessedness were not meant for me, and that all the happiness and joy I hitherto had was really only borrowed sunshine from the parsonage. And with the sin I was carrying, I could only have Susanna as a loan until I died, when we should have to part, and I must go back to the evil powers of unhappiness, which, from my earliest hour here at home, had taken possession of me.

I leant against the wall and cried.

As I was about to continue my dressing, and turned to the glass, it was without terror, even with a certain tranquility, that my gaze fell on the old vision of my childhood, the lady with the rose whom I saw standing behind me in the open chamber-door, pale and sorrowful, looking at me, until she suddenly vanished.

The church bells were ringing and the people were streaming towards the church. Today Anne Kvæn and all the house servants were also among the churchgoers. Father went with me, and bowed respectfully to the minister when they met at the entrance.

The order in which we confirmation candidates were to stand in church had been decided the Monday before. I was to stand first on the boys' side, Susanna first on the girls' side.

One hymn had already been sung before Susanna came with her mother, dressed like a grown-up lady in a black silk dress, with gauze on her neck and arms, and a locket on her breast. She remained sitting by her mother in the parsonage pew until the affecting sermon was over.

I must have looked very ill and exhausted; for as the minister began the catechizing at me, he stopped in the middle of a question with a look as if asking what was the matter with me. I answered his question correctly, and with a nod he went across to Susanna, who stood there with folded hands, looking down, tearful and rather pale with excitement before her question came. While her father put it, she looked up at him with her sweet blue eyes so innocently and trustfully that it was more than clear that she had no thought of an evil conscience at that moment. When it was got through and her father went on to the next candidate, she smiled, relieved though serious, across to me as if I were the person to whom she could properly turn in this hour.

I looked, as often as I could do so unnoticed, across to her as she stood there, tall and beautiful, with her luxuriant hair dressed in grown-up fashion. Now and then she looked across at me, but I avoided meeting her eye. Her glance now seemed to add to my sin, just as every sacred word I heard only added to my load, and had an effect the very opposite of comforting.

The service was long, and the nervous strain affected me, as it has often done since, in such a way that there was a singing in my ears and dark spots swam before my eyes. Wherever I looked there appeared to my horror a dark blot, and, full of anxiety, I thought that perhaps this was already the beginning of the curse. I dared not look at Susanna anymore for fear of throwing the black spot on her, and at last I could not forbear looking at the floor where I stood to see if there were possibly burned marks under my feet. I thought of the sea-sprite, who in Vaagen's church had enticed the minister's daughter to go with him, and whose instinct had driven him out of church during the blessing, whereas I was condemned to stand.

After the promise was given, I remember only dimly that another discourse was pronounced and more hymns were sung.

When I once more found myself upon the way home with my father, who with an anxious look supported me, my last recollection of the whole thing was that Susanna, who I suppose discovered that I was ill, had towards the end of the service looked at me with just the same expression as the lady with the rose had done that very morning – quiet, pale, sorrowful, like one who would be glad to help, but could not.

I think that what my father had said to me about not disgracing him before the minister contributed not a little to the fact that I kept up to the last; for I fainted as soon as we got home and was put to bed, while my father, who had now become seriously alarmed, immediately sent an express messenger for the doctor.

When he came the next day, he found me in wild delirium. My fancy overflowed, like a river from which all dams are removed, with a stream of the wildest conceptions. It seemed to me that dreadful forms danced and nodded round the bed, and among them one with a long letter of condemnation, with a seal under it, and that Anne Kvæn was there, rolling glittering eyes, while now and again Susanna looked at me with a glance full of pain, as if it were not in her power to hinder my perdition.

From what I learned afterwards, the doctor at first thought it was a nervous fever, but from certain symptoms and the nature of my ravings, concerning which Anne Kvæn, who probably had her own thoughts on the subject, thought it necessary to inform him, he quite changed his opinion. He had attended my poor mother in her mental illness, and now found the same fancy about the lady and the rose, and the same dread of evil spirits in me the son.

Three weeks later I was quite well again, though pale and exhausted by the long nervous paroxysms. The whole millstone weight of sin was, as it were, gone from my bosom, and I went to the altar without the smallest scruple.

And I felt quite a dignified person when, on the following Sunday, I went on a confirmation visit to the parsonage in my black dress-coat. On this occasion Susanna sat – perhaps a little on show on my account – like a grown-up lady at her own work-table in the window-seat. When her mother went out of the room to fetch red-currant wine and cakes,

I, at a sign from her, had hastily to look at her precious work-table with all the drawers, both those above and those that appeared below when she pushed the upper drawers away. In one of these last, which she opened with an arch look, but shut again like lightning as her mother came in, lay the brass ring with glass stones in it that I had once given her, and I recognized two or three old scraps of letters dating from the time when we were children.

When I went away it was with a beating heart, for I had unexpectedly an interview in which Susanna's true feeling had been revealed to me more clearly than it could have been by any verbal assurance.

It struck me that something must lately have happened at home, for the curt, cold way in which my father used to treat me was wonderfully changed. For instance, he made me a present of a double-barreled gun in a sealskin case, and a watch, and he proposed that during the days before my going away Jens and the four-oared boat should be at my disposal as often as I wished to go out shooting or fishing.

I understood what had happened when the doctor one day made his appearance, and asked me to go up with him to my room.

The broadly-built, bald, little doctor, in his homespun coat, and steel-rimmed spectacles on his snub-nose, was one of the hardy people of our fjord districts who glory in going out in all kinds of weather. You always saw him in the best of spirits when he had just been out in stormy weather. He was a decided and clear-headed man, whose manner involuntarily inspired confidence, and he also possessed a warmth and open-heartedness that made him, when he chose, very winning. He was the doctor both at our house and the parsonage, and a confidential friend of both families.

When we came up to my room, he told me to sit down and listen to him, while he himself, as usual, made out a route on the floor, where, with his hands behind him, he could walk up and down while he talked.

He had, he said, considered carefully whether he should conceal from me what he had on his mind, or speak out as he was now doing, but had decided on the latter course, as my recovery depended upon my being perfectly clear as to what it was I was suffering from. My last illness had, partly at any rate, been an outbreak of a disposition to insanity, which he knew lay in the family on my mother's side for several generations back. That this outbreak had now taken place in me was certainly due to the fact that I had given myself up to all kinds of imaginary influences, in conjunction with the idle life which he knew I had always led at home. The only certain means for stopping the development of this disposition was work with a fixed, determined end in view – for instance, study – which he thought I showed an ability for, and in addition a healthy life – walks, hunting, fishing, companions and interests; but no more idleness, no more exciting novels, no more unhealthy dreams. He had talked to my father upon the subject, and recommended that I should go to the training college at Trondenæs as a fitting preparation for study, and as a measure that would also afford the necessary interruption to my present life.

When the doctor soon after left me, I remained sitting in my room, serious and much moved.

That I had thus become transparent to myself, and had solved my own riddle, was an extraordinary relief to me – I may say it was an episode in my life.

The feeling of being mentally ill, which had always, as long as I could remember, lain a silent pressure, a foreboding of unhappiness, in the background of my mind – although dissipated in the brighter summer-time of my companionship with Susanna – was therefore no sin, no burden of crime, no dark mysterious exception in me from every other natural order of things, but only a disease, actually only a disease, which was to be treated with a correspondingly natural treatment!

I had never thought that anyone could be as glad to hear that he was mad, or at any rate that there was danger of his becoming so, as overgood news; but now I know that such a thing can be.

I prayed now, as it seemed for the first time in my life, really, confidently, and trustfully to God, to whom I stood in the same relation as everyone else, or, if there were any difference, even nearer, because I was a poor, sick creature.

I felt as if God's sun had shone out upon me after a long, weary, rainy day. I prayed for myself, for Susanna, for my father; and in the enjoyment of this new condition of security I went on to pray first for every single person at home, then for those at the parsonage, then for the clerk, and at last, for want of others, as we do in church, for "all who are sick and sorrowful," among whom, with a glad heart, I now classed myself.

# Chapter VI

## AT THE CLERK'S

It was only two days before I was to start for Trondenæs in a vessel which was lying ready to go north.

While I was irresolutely considering every possible means of getting a last talk with Susanna before I started, there came a message from the clerk to say that I must be sure to come out to him the next day at eleven o'clock precisely; he would not be at home later.

The same morning that the message came Susanna had been at the clerk's. Without saying a word, she sat down at the table with her face buried in her arms.

When the alarmed clerk pressed the "child of his heart" – as he called her in his concern – for an explanation, she at length lifted up a tear-stained face to him, and said she was crying because she was so very, very unhappy.

"But why, dear Susanna?"

"Because," burst suddenly on his ear, "I love David, and he loves me, and we are engaged; but no one must know it except you – and you will not betray us?"

With this last question she threw herself weeping upon the neck of the stunned and bewildered clerk, who in his heart was already won over, long before he had made out what it was he was undertaking.

He replaced Susanna in her chair, talked to her and comforted her until he had matured in his own mind the sensible reply, that we ought to look upon the coming two years of separation as trial years, and therefore, during that time, we ought not to write to one another. Only, he had to promise in return that we should meet the next morning at his house for a few moments, for a last farewell, and that, during the time I was away, he should tell her everything he heard about me.

When I came to him the next day, I found him sitting on a wooden chair, very serious and thoughtful, with his arms supported on his knees, and staring down at the floor, which was strewn with juniper, as if for a grand occasion. My arrival did not seem to disturb his reflections, although a little nod when I entered showed me that at any rate I was noticed. He swung his violin slowly backwards and forwards before his knees, with a gentle twang of the strings at each swing, so that it sounded like a far-off church bell. His gentle grey eyes rested on me with a pondering, critical gaze, as if he were really looking at me now for the first time, and a faint smile showed that the examination had not a bad result.

A little while after, a shadow crossed the doorway, and to my surprise Susanna came in. She came quickly up to me, blushing, and took my hand, saying:

"Dear David, the clerk knows everything; he has given us leave to say good-bye here."

"Yes, children, I have," said the clerk, "but only for a few moments, because Susanna begged so hard for it, and also that you may both hear my opinion of the whole thing after thinking it over."

He now made a little speech, in which he said that he did not see anything very wrong in our loving one another, although we were indeed absurdly young. He hoped, too – and he had thought a great deal about it – that our not revealing our engagement to our parents was excusable, as they would scarcely even look at the matter as really serious, and we might feel hurt. He did not intend to be a receiver of secret love-letters, as Susanna had asked him, and that both for his own sake and for ours, because we ought to use the approaching two years of trial to see if there really were any truth in our love, or if it were only a childish fancy of the kind that afterwards evaporates.

With these words the old clerk good-naturedly left the room.

When we were alone, Susanna told me in a whisper why she had ventured to confide in the clerk. She had heard at home that in his youth he had once been disappointed in love, and that that was the reason why he had never married, and had become so strange. Then in eager haste she drew out of her pocket – she still wore her old, short, blue-checked, everyday dress, but her hair "in grown-up fashion" – a cross of small, blue beads. She also drew from her pocket a silk cord which I was to wear round my neck nearest my heart.

With some further trouble she produced from the pocket that contained so much, a small pair of scissors. With these she cut off a curl of my hair, just that black one on the temple, that she had long had her eye upon, she said, and which she meant to keep in her confirmation locket. When I asked for one of hers that I "had long had my eye upon," she said it was not necessary, as the bead cross she had given me was threaded on her own hair.

Then there was something I must promise her, which she had thought out while she sat sewing at home, for she thought of so much then. It was, that when I became a student, I should give her a gold engagement ring with the inscription "David and Susanna" on one half of the inside, and on the other half there should be "like David and Jonathan." It was the disagreement between our parents that had made her think of this.

"But," she broke off, "you are not listening to me, David?"

And, indeed, I was thinking about something else, and that was, whether I dared give her a farewell kiss: I remembered last summer out among the Vætte Rocks.

At that moment there was a scraping of feet on the doorstep outside, which meant that the clerk thought our interview must soon come to an end, and, to my disappointment, Susanna hastened to hide the presents, which I still held in my hand, in my breast pocket. She had just done this when the clerk came in, and said that now we must say good-bye to one another.

Susanna looked at the clerk, and then, pale, and with eyes full of tears, at me, as if the thought that we were to part now struck her for the first time. She made a quick movement – she evidently wanted to throw her arms round my neck, but restrained herself, because the clerk was present.

So she only took my hand, lifted it to her lips without saying a word and hurried away.

It was more than I could bear, and I think it was too much for the old clerk too. He walked up and down, gently twanging his violin strings, while I, at the table, let my tears flow freely.

Before I left he played a beautiful little piece which he had composed when he was twenty. It touched me deeply, because I felt as if it were written about Susanna and me; it echoed long after in my mind, so that I learnt it by heart.

"There is a continuation of it," said he, when he had ended, and then – after a short pause as of sad recollection – "but it is not very cheerful, and is not suitable for you!"

The next morning early, when the yacht sailed, a handkerchief was waved from the drawing room window in the parsonage, and, in answer, a glazed hat was lifted on board.

# Chapter VII
## TRONDENÆS

On a naze to the north of Hind Island in Sengen lies Trondenæs church and parsonage. The latter was a royal palace in Saint Olaf's time, and Thore Hund's brother Siver lived there. Bjark Island, where Thore Hund had his castle, is only a few miles off.

The church itself is in many respects a remarkable historical monument. Its two towers, of which one was square and covered with copper, and had an iron spire, and the other octagonal, exist only in legends, and of the famous "three wonderfully high, equal-sized statues" there are only remains which are to be seen at the west doorway.

This church was once the most northern border-fortress of Christendom, and stood grandly with its white towers, the far-echoing tones of its bells and its sacred song, like a giant bishop in white surplice, who bore St. Olaf's consecration and altar lights into the darkness among the Finmark trolls. Its power over men's minds has been correspondingly deep and great. Thither past generations for miles round have wended in Sunday dress before other churches were built up there. If the soapstone font which stands in the choir could enumerate the names of those baptized at it, or the altar the bridal pairs that have been married there, or the venerable church itself tell what it knew, we should hear many a strange tale.

Protestantism has plundered the church there as elsewhere; remains of its painted altar-shrines are found as doors to the peasants' cupboards, and what was most imposing about the building is in ruins. But the work of destruction could not be carried farther. The old Roman Catholic church feeling surrounds it to a certain extent to this day, with the old legends that float around it, and is kept up by the foreign paintings in the choir, by the mystical vaults, and by all the ruins, which the Nordlander's imagination builds up into indistinct grandeur. The poor man there is, moreover, a Catholic in no small degree in his religious mode of thought and in his superstition. It comes quite naturally to him, in deadly peril, to promise a wax candle to the church, or to offer prayer to the Virgin Mary. He knows well enough that she is dethroned, but nevertheless he piously includes her in his devotions.

I dwell upon the memories of this church and its surroundings, because during the two years I stayed at Trondenæs I was so strongly influenced by their power over the imagination. The hollow ground with the supposed underground vaults were to me like a covered abyss, full of mysteries, and in the church – whose silence I often sought, since it lies, with its strangely thought-absorbing interior, close to the parsonage, and, as a rule, stood open on account of the college organ practice – daylight sometimes cast shadows in the aisles and niches as if beings from another age were moving about.

I made great progress in Latin and Greek under the teaching of the agreeable, well-informed minister, in whose house I lived, and in other subjects under one of the masters of the college; but in my leisure hours I sought the spots which gave so much occupation to my fancy, and therefore Trondenæs was anything but the right place for my diseased mind.

My nervous excitability has some connection with the moon's changes as I have since noticed. At such times the church exercised an almost irresistible fascination over me; I stole there unnoticed and alone, and would sit for hours lost in thought over one thing and another, indistinct creations of my imagination, and among them Susanna's light form, which sometimes seemed to float towards me, without my ever being quite able to see her face.

It was late in the spring of the second year I was at Trondenæs, that one midday, being under the influence of one of these unhealthy moods, I sat in the church on a raised place near the high altar, meditating, with Susanna's blue cross in my hand.

My eye fell on a large dark picture on the wall beside the altar, which I had often seen, but without its having made any special impression on me. It represented in life-size a martyr who has been cast into a thorn-bush; the sharp thorns, as long as daggers, pierced his body in all directions, and he could not utter a complaint, because one great sharp thorn went into his throat and out at his open mouth.

The expression of this face struck me all at once as terrible. It regarded me with a look of silent understanding, as though I were a companion in suffering, and would have to lie there when its torments had at last come to an end. It was impossible to remove my eyes from the picture; it seemed to become alive, now coming quite near, now going far away into a darkness that my own dizzy head created.

It was as though in this picture the curtain was drawn aside from a part of my own soul's secret history, and it was only by an effort of will, called forth by a fear of becoming too far absorbed into my own fancy, that I succeeded in tearing myself away from it.

When I turned, there stood in the light that fell from the window near the front pew, the lady with the rose. She wore an expression of infinite sadness, as though she knew well the connection between me and the picture, and as if the briar-spray in her hand were only a miniature of the thorn-bush in which yonder martyr lay.

In the lonely stillness of the church a panic came over me, an inexpressible terror of unseen powers, and I fled precipitately.

When I got outside, I discovered that I had lost Susanna's blue cross. It could only be in the church on the step where I had been sitting. At that moment, while my heart was still throbbing with terror, I would not have gone back again into the church for anything in the world – except Susanna's blue cross. I found it, when I carefully searched the floor where I had been sitting.

The second time during these years that my nervous system gave evidence of its unsoundness was late in the autumn, a month or two before I was to go home.

A peasant, who had gone in to see the minister, had fastened his horse, which was wall-eyed, to the churchyard wall. I began to look at it; and the recollection of its dead, expressionless glance followed me for the rest of the day. It seemed to me as if its eyes, instead of looking out, looked inwards into a world invisible to me, and as if it would be quite natural if it forgot to obey the reins, and left the ordinary highway for the road to Hades, along which the dead are traveling.

With this in my mind, I sat that afternoon in the parsonage where people were talking of all kinds of things, and there suddenly appeared before me a home face, pale and with a strained look, and soon after I could see that the man to whom it belonged was striving desperately to climb up from the raging surf on to a rock. It was no other than our man Anders. He fixed his dull, glassy eyes upon me as he struggled, apparently hindered from saving himself by something down at his feet, which I could not see. He looked as if he wanted to tell me something. The vision only lasted a moment; but a torturing almost unbearable feeling, that in the same moment some misfortune was befalling us at home, drove me from the room to wander restlessly in the fields for the rest of the day.

When I came back they asked me what had been the matter, that I had so suddenly turned deadly pale and hurried from the room.

A fortnight later there came a sad letter from home. My father's yacht, the *Hope,* which, after the custom of those days, was not insured, and was loaded for the most part with fish, which my father had bought at his own cost, had been wrecked on the way from Bergen in a storm on Stadt Sea. The ship had sprung a leak, and late in the afternoon had to be run ashore. The crew had escaped with their lives, but our man Anders had had both legs broken.

This shipwreck gave the first decided blow to my father's fortune. The second was to come towards the end of the following year, in the loss of another yacht, the *Unity*; and the third blow, with more important results, was struck when it was at last decided by Government that our trading station was not to be a stopping-place for steamers.

# Chapter VIII
## AT HOME

In December I was once more at home, where I found everything outwardly the same as of old, only, possibly by reason of what had passed, still quieter and sadder. My father was restlessly active, but not very communicative. He probably did not consider me fitted to share his anxieties.

Susanna, who, like myself, was now over nineteen years of age, was on a visit at a house some miles away and was to come home at Christmas. My longing for her was indescribable.

It was during the last dark, stormy week before Christmas, that the Spanish brig *Sancta Maria* was driven by the weather in to our station, in a rather damaged condition, which, with the poor labor we could command, resulted in her having to lie under repair for nearly six weeks.

The captain, who owned both ship and cargo, was a tall, sallow, becomingly-dressed Spaniard, with iron-grey hair, black eyes, and large features. With him was his son, Antonio Martinez, a handsome young man with an olive-brown face and fiery eyes like his father's.

My father, who had done Señor Martinez considerable service in the getting in the cargo, now invited him, with Nordland hospitality, to put up at our house.

Although the intercourse between us could not be very lively, as the foreigners only understood a few Norwegian words and were often obliged to have recourse to a phrase-book, it was soon evident that they were both very agreeable men. Their principal occupation consisted in making and smoking cigarettes the whole day, and in superintending the work on the brig.

The dark season has a depressing effect upon the spirits of many in the North, especially on those days when there is very little to do. Thus, during Christmas, and especially on Christmas Eve, my father used to be excessively melancholy. While gaiety filled the whole house, and the smartly-dressed servants kept Christmas round the kitchen table, which was adorned with treble-branched candlesticks, he generally sat shut up in the office with his own thoughts, and would not be disturbed by anyone.

This Christmas Eve, however, he was in the parlor for a while, on Señor Martinez's account; but he was silent and dejected the whole time, as if he were only longing for his solitary office, to which, moreover, he retired directly after supper.

# Chapter IX
## THE CHRISTMAS VISIT

About Christmas-time that winter in our part of Lofoten there were a number of foreigners, mostly ships' captains, who, on account of bad weather or damage to their vessels, were staying at different places on shore, as Martinez was with us. There were also notabilities from the south on public business. One result of this was a number of social gatherings, in which the hosts vied with one another in open hospitality.

On the third New Year's day[*] we were invited to dinner and a ball at the house of the wealthy magistrate, Röst, where some of the gentlemen from the south were staying for the time. It was only a journey of a mile and a half[†] for us, but many had six or eight miles to go, and the greater part of that by sea.

Röst's large rooms could accommodate a great number of guests, but this time, in order to put up for the night all those invited, he had had to take a neighboring house in addition.

In proceeding with the account of this visit, which was to be so eventful and exciting for me, I have promised myself to be short, and shall thus omit many a feature and many an outline that belongs to a more detailed representation of the life in Nordland.

According to the invitation, we were to dine at three, but most of the boats made their appearance two or three hours in advance of that time. While the ladies were dressing upstairs, the gentlemen assembled in an intentionally dimly-lighted room, where they could take a "mouthful" and a dram, which were very acceptable after the journey. They were also made acquainted with one another by the careful host.

We waited long and in vain for the minister and his ladies, and at last had to go to table without them.

---

* The 3rd of January.

† Between ten and eleven English miles.

The doors of the large, brilliantly-lighted dining room were now thrown open, the guests streamed upstairs, and, after much stopping in the doorway and long polite disputes over the order of precedence, took their places round the great loaded horse-shoe table, that glittered gaily with a compact row of wine bottles, treble-branched candlesticks, high cake-dishes, and, especially up by the place of honor, a perfect heap of massive silver plate. Three places were reserved for the minister and his family up by the notabilities. My father sat by Señor Martinez at the principal table, and I, in modesty, farther down at one of the side tables.

The dinner was of that good, old, genial sort which is now unfortunately going more and more out of fashion. It is true, people ate with their knives and knew nothing about silver forks; but on the other hand there was real happiness in the gathering, and it formed the subject of many an entertaining conversation for long after.

At first, while we were still chilled by the cold feeling of the white cloth, and awed by the festal atmosphere, it was indeed very stiff. Neighbors scarcely ventured to whisper to one another, and the young ladies in ball-dresses, who, as if by a magnetic cohesion, were all together, sat for a long time in a row in deep, embarrassed silence, like a hedge of blue, red, and white flowers, in which no bird dared sing.

The dinner began by the host bidding his guests welcome. He next proposed in succession the healths of the notabilities present in rather long, prepared speeches, which were responded to by them.

After this everyone felt that they had passed over the official threshold to enjoyment.

The host, with lightened heart, now entered upon the much shorter and simpler toasts for the absent, among whom, first and foremost, was the "good minister and his family." Several besides myself noticed that my father left his glass untouched at this toast.

In the meantime the courses went round, and as the level of the wine in the bottles sank, the gaiety rose. Many a quick, sharp brain that here found its own ground now came to the fore, and the falling hail of jests and witty and amusing sayings – the last generally in the form of stories with a point that was sometimes, perhaps, rather coarse – gave a lively impression of the peculiar Nordland humor.

It was only what, at that time, usually happened at parties, when the company leave the table, that there were a few who could not rise from their chairs, and others who, as a result of the attempt, were afterwards missing. Among the latter I was unfortunately classed.

The impression of the moment has always had a great power over me, and, unaccustomed as I was both to this kind of gaiety and to strong drink, I had surrendered myself without a thought to the mirth that buzzed around me. I think I never laughed so much in my whole life together as I did at that dinner-table. Nearly opposite to me sat the red-haired merchant Wadel, with his long, dryly comical face, firing off one witticism after another, and at my side whispered the hump-backed clerk Gram, who was famed for his cleverness, and feared for his biting tongue. His sharp remarks upon the different people who sat at the table, grew in ill-nature as he drank, and if his words had been heard, the expression of many a beaming face would certainly have changed. I believe, also, that he took a secret pleasure in trying to make me intoxicated; at any rate he was unwearied in filling my glass, especially when the heating wines began to go round. His quick, sharp snake's-eyes and a few whispered words directed my now thoroughly beclouded attention to many a comical scene around me.

At length it seemed to me that the room and the table were going up and down, as if we were sitting in a large cabin in rough weather. I also remember indistinctly that afterwards in the moving room we squeezed past each other, round the table, between the wall and the chairs, in two opposite streams, and thanked our hosts for the dinner.*

After all this I remember nothing, until I awoke, in total darkness, as if out of a heavy confused dream, and felt that I was lying in a soft eider-down bed. Little by little all that had passed dawned upon my recollection, and I comprehended that I had been put to bed in one of the guest-chambers in the neighboring house.

While I lay pondering over this, and feeling intensely unhappy, the elder Señor Martinez came in with a candle in his hand to look after me. It then appeared that it was past two o'clock in the morning, and to the circumstance that I had thus slept six or seven hours in succession I probably owed the fact that I no longer felt any physical indisposition; but morally I suffered all the more from a feeling of shame.

As far as I could understand, as I dressed myself, the house had been turned into a perfect lazaretto for the same class of fallen after dinner as myself, and among them I noticed, with a kind of revengeful joy, Gram the clerk, my hump-backed mischievous neighbor.

Señor Martinez made known to me, by all kinds of spirited gesticulations, that dancing was now going on briskly, and that I must join the dancers.

The thought that Susanna must have come long ago, and must have been waiting in vain, shot like lightning through my mind. How I could have forgotten her, though even for an instant, was a riddle; but the fact

* It is a Norwegian custom to shake hands with and thank the host and hostess, after a meal, for the hospitality of which one has partaken. Children in the same way always thank their parents.

that I had done so weighed heavily upon me.

The dining room was now transformed into a ballroom, and dancing had already been going on merrily for several hours to the sound of violin, clarinet, and violoncello. At an opportune moment, in the middle of a dance, I slipped in unnoticed.

At first, as I stood in my tight white kid gloves, pale and embarrassed, down by the open door through which the heat streamed out into the cold passage like a mist, I suffered very much from the feeling that everyone would look at me and remember my unseemly behavior.

Couple after couple glided past, so near that the ladies' dresses touched me, and gradually I began, as far as my near sight would allow, to find my bearings in the room.

The minister's wife sat on the sofa, farthest up among some elderly ladies, in earnest conversation with the little bald doctor.

The minister was probably playing cards downstairs; but of Susanna I saw nothing.

At the upper end of the room, young Martinez, with a beaming face, was just dancing a polka with a strikingly beautiful girl dressed in white, with a fluttering blue ribbon round her waist. She had thick beautiful hair of a shade nearly golden, with a large silver pin like a dart run through it, and a light wreath. The lady was taller and fuller in figure than Susanna, but with a certain grace that reminded me of her. The light, almost fashionably delicate way in which she placed her small feet in dancing – it was as though she floated – also resembled Susanna, and I therefore followed the pair with unconscious interest.

My short sight prevented me from distinguishing well, and as they passed me, the lady's bent head was hidden by her own arm, which rested confidingly on the shoulder of the evidently happy Martinez. What I saw was only a broad, pure, innocent brow, which could belong to but one person in the world, and that an escaped lock of hair played upon the round white shoulder.

I felt my knees tremble. This tall, elegant, distinguished lady could never be Susanna!

With a feeling of jealousy I watched the pair intently until the next time they came by. When just opposite to me the lady raised her eyes, her glance fell upon me, and a deep blush suddenly overspread her face and neck right down to the lace edging on her dress.

It was Susanna!

During the scarcely more than two years that we had been separated her beauty had developed wonderfully. The tender seventeen-year-old girl-bud had developed into a splendid full-grown woman.

The pair sat down at the top of the room near the row of elderly ladies.

I saw next that these two were going through the last long-dance of the ball, the cotillion, which is generally varied by an endless number of figures, and the thought darted through my mind, that probably young Martinez had been winning favor with Susanna the whole evening, since he was now her partner in this particular dance. I noticed how the minister's wife paid him marked attention, and I reflected bitterly that he was both a rich man, and also, though shorter in stature, looked much more grown-up and manly than I.

A knife seemed to go through my heart. I had been lying intoxicated, like a beast, and allowed a stranger to take Susanna from me.

With wild jealousy I noticed how the handsome Martinez, dumb, but speaking with his dark, fiery eyes, was trying, amid laughter and all kinds of lively nods and gestures, to explain to Susanna a new figure which was just going to begin, how he sometimes bent over her, as if whispering confidentially, and how she, from her seat, looked up at him and laughed merrily, as only Susanna could laugh. He took her hand and made her try the step on the floor in front of their seats, and this seemed to be even more amusing.

Young Martinez evidently engrossed her, and I feared she perhaps thought our old relations were only childish fancies, which as a grown-up woman she now wished forgotten. She might consider that after our agreement about the two trial years, everything between us was to be at an end, so that, as grown-up people we could talk and laugh over the whole affair without misunderstanding each other.

My blood boiled, and I felt that I must revenge myself. Before I had quite considered how, I began, with a sudden inspiration, to converse eagerly with Merchant R.'s pretty daughter, who happened to be standing close to me, so that it might appear as if I were paying court to her.

When presently Susanna passed us in the new figure, she looked in a wondering, questioning way at me. The next time she passed, she inadvertently dropped her handkerchief just at the place where I stood. I picked it up, went up the room, and stiffly handed it to the minister's wife, who – in consequence either of my behavior at the dinner-table, or of something else – received me with marked reserve and coldness. I bowed as coldly to her, and then returned to my old place, where I resumed the interrupted lively conversation with Miss R.

Shortly after, Susanna again came past, and this time looked at me with a serious, but uncertain expression, as if she could not quite make up her mind what to think; after that she purposely dropped her eyes every time she passed me.

I discovered to my satisfaction that Martinez really danced clumsily.

While I talked with forced gaiety to my pretty companion, I was secretly tempted, all unnoticed, to put out my foot, a little ill-naturedly, so that he should trip over it. And I do not quite know how it happened, but the next time Martinez passed, he fell full length on the floor, and must have hurt himself considerably; in falling, however, he was gallant enough to let go the support he might have had in his partner, so that Susanna only half fell.

He rose, and looked angrily at me, the innocent cause of the mishap, who was apparently too much engrossed in my neighbor to have even noticed what was going on. The look he received in return for his, however, revealed to him, though involuntarily, the whole truth; for he was in the act of rushing at me, when he was unexpectedly stopped by Susanna, a trifle pale, stepping in front of him, and, with the bearing of a woman of the world, quietly stretching out her hand for him to conduct her farther.

As Susanna went arm in arm up the room with the limping Martinez, she suddenly turned her face to me with a look so beaming with joy, that from deep despair I was suddenly raised to the happiest, most exulting certainty.

She had evidently understood that Martinez's misfortune was an act of revenge on my part, for her sake, and her mind was thereby relieved of the doubt which my conduct for the last hour must have occasioned her; for she had soon seen that I was not intoxicated, and coquetry was a thing too far from her own sincere, truthful nature for her to be able to imagine it in me. In perfect truthfulness, she was really only a refined, feminine edition of her father's strong nature.

I went and made repeated apologies to young Martinez for my awkwardness, while Susanna sat by and listened, and at length, good-natured as in reality he was, he consented to be appeased. His face did grow rather long when, immediately after, Susanna proposed that I should lead her through the figure now going on, so that he could rest his injured leg for the next.

Yes, I danced with her, a beautiful, full-grown woman in the white ball-dress, whom a short while ago I had not recognized, because her own splendidly developed beauty hid her.

We had taught one another to dance, and I think we both danced unusually well. The light wreath with its delicate white flowers, set off the beauty of her luxuriant hair; my arm was round her waist, and I felt how yieldingly she leant upon me, happy and trusting as a child, as we swayed in the dance. Her forehead was near my lips, and as our eyes sought each other's during the dance, they said again and again, how delightful it was to meet, when we had longed so for one another for two whole years.

When I took her back to her place I received a pressure of the hand and a look, which made me completely invulnerable to the less friendly glances of her mother. It appeared that Susanna was then reprimanded for her neglect of the young Señor Martinez, but the doctor, who sat beside her, spoke in her defense.

I stood once more in my old place, and saw Susanna and Martinez go through the next figure.

Her curling lip showed at first a trace of the old childish defiance after reproof; but soon her expression became more tranquil and thoughtful.

Taken up as I was with the sight of her; and possibly weak after the many and varied emotions I had experienced, I suddenly felt the oppressive, uneasy sense of terror and misfortune come over me, which generally accompanies my visions. I attempted to leave the room, but the vision was upon me before I could do so.

I saw Susanna's face while she danced with Martinez, as white as that of a strikingly beautiful corpse, and the green wreath with the small white flowers hung in her hair like wet sea-grass. It seemed as if water were streaming down her.

The blood rushed to my heart; the room was now dark, amid sparks from thousands of lights, going round before my eyes with the dancing pair.

I should certainly have fainted at the door, had not the doctor taken me by the arm, and led me out into the cool passage, and from thence into a little guest-chamber, where he made me drink some water and lie down on the bed.

When he came back, half an hour after the attack, and saw that I had recovered, he sat down by me on the bed, gentle and friendly, and began in his sincere way to speak out, as he said.

As he thoughtfully unraveled with the snuffers the wick of the candle which he had in his hand, having taken it from the dressing-table, in order, I suppose, to observe me, he said he had noticed me this evening, from the time I came into the room, and thought that my fancy inclined to the beautiful Susanna L., but that I was jealous of young Martinez. He had also heard a little bird sing about this before.

It was a feeling which many young people would only be the better for and be developed by, but for me, with my mental disposition, this kind of exciting idea was harmful in the highest degree; he had, he gently added, unfortunately had experience of this in the case of my own poor mother; for her discovery, in my childhood, that I had inherited her mental disease, had only been the accidental cause of her loss of reason.

As a physician and a friend he would now say this, while he thought there was still time for me to prevent this fancy taking root. And he would say it not only for my own sake, but also for Susanna's, for he was very fond of her, and would very unwillingly see her led into what, from a human point of view, could only end in sorrow.

One thing I must consider, he continued – after a long pause, during which he seemed to be considering whether he should say all he had to say, and finally decided upon doing so – and that was, that my unfortunate hereditary disposition did not allow of my thinking of marriage; it might, he went on with a gesture, as if performing a last, decisive operation on the candle, even be regarded in the same light as if a leper married without heeding that he thereby transmitted his disease to his children. I must not, however – here he rose and laid his hand consolingly on my shoulder – take these things too much to heart. The most bitter remedies – and unfortunately the truth was such – are generally the wholesomest, and for my sick, dreaming nature, he thought, after earnest, mature consideration, that the unvarnished truth was the only means of giving health and salvation.

After once more holding up the candle over me, he retired with, a serious nod; be could easily see that for the moment I was not in a condition to carry on any conversation, or give him any answer.

It was, in all friendliness, the death-blow to all my dreams and illusions.

I felt stunned by the blow, although my inward understanding had not yet taken it in clearly. My life's old foreboding of misfortune was now at last confirmed. Susanna had therefore, for me, been but borrowed sunshine now, and my hopes were to be extinguished forever.

I lay perfectly calm, rather seeing this with my mind's eye than thinking it, while the music sounded faintly from the ballroom, and little by little I felt myself with a dull pain die away, as it were, from everything that was dear to me in the world. My body seemed to stiffen under the sorrow, and Susanna's face, without a gleam of life in it, stood before me like something unnatural: my love was a dead history.

As I still lay in a dull, motionless stupor, through which everything without appeared to me in a half mist, the door opened, and a lady came in. She began hastily to repair with pins before the mirror a rent in her dress, but suddenly stopped, alarmed at seeing someone in the half-darkness lying on the bed.

I recognized Susanna, and, as it seemed to me, something told her that it must be I who lay there, for she approached as if to see, and whispered my name.

She probably thought I was asleep, as no answer came, and that it was neither right nor the time to wake me. She stood by me for a moment as if considering, then bent over me till I felt her warm breath, gently kissed my forehead, and went out.

A Christmas visit in northern districts generally lasts a couple of days, often more. But, as my father and the Martinezes had so much to do and our house was not very far, we were to go home as early as the next evening, while most of the others were to wait until the following day.

The minister's family, however, were to remain as guests, together with the "notabilities," to the end of the week. In the meantime, as, early the next day, the minister and his wife were going to call on a family in the neighborhood, Susanna had to stay at the magistrate's house.

I, like the other guests, had not risen until far on in the morning, but in my brain during all the time Dr. K.'s words about my position being like that of a leper had throbbed as a boil, growing harder and more painful with my changing ideas on the subject, until all at once their meaning stood clear with its whole sting before me.

I loved Susanna a thousand times more than myself, and should I selfishly wish to unite her fate to a man who was insane, only because that man was myself? And perhaps my mental condition would grow worse as time went on.

I began to feel within me a pious courage for self-sacrifice, and with it came calm, soothing peacefulness. When all was said and done, it was really the best thing I could think of, to give my life for Susanna, and this thought at last inspired me with an almost fanatical wish to do so.

My mind was made up; and my plan was the simple one of speaking out decidedly and clearly to her; for I would not for all the world deceive her in any way.

It was in the afternoon, in the twilight, while the others were out for a walk, that I found an opportunity of talking to her alone.

That day Susanna had on a black silk dress which fitted her to perfection, a lace collar and narrow sleeves with cuffs at the wrists. Her hair was fastened with a silver arrow as at the ball, but it was her only ornament.

She sat thoughtfully listening to me in front of the newly-lighted stove where we had placed ourselves. Every time she bent forward into the light from the stove door, it fell upon her expressive face, while I, in my endeavor to be true, told her, possibly with exaggerated coloring, all about my mental condition, and what Dr. K. had said.

As I talked I saw her face growing paler and more and more serious, until at last, leaning her elbows on her knees, she covered her eyes with her hands so that I could only see that her lips were trembling and that she was crying.

When I came to what the doctor had said about my condition resembling that of a leper, and that thus God Himself had placed an obstacle in the way of our union, while I tried consolingly to represent to her that for the whole of our life, with the exception of the last two years, we had really loved one another in a different way, like brother and sister – she suddenly raised her head in wild defiance, so that I could look straight into her tear-stained face, threw her arms around my neck and forced me down on my knees in front of her. She pressed my head close up to her throbbing heart as if she would defend me against all who wanted to injure me. Then with her hand she stroked the hair back from my forehead – I felt her tears falling on my face – and she repeated caressingly again and again as if in delirium, that no one in the world should take me from her.

This was too much for my weary, suffering heart; I seized both her hands in mine and cried over them, with my head in her lap. My weeping grew more violent, until at last it rose to a desperate, convulsive sobbing, which I could no longer control, and which thoroughly alarmed Susanna; for she hushed me, called me by my name, and kissed me like a child, to quiet me. I felt such a deep need of having my cry out, that it could not now be stopped.

When at last I became quieter she once more clasped her hands about my neck, as if to compel my attention, bent forward, and looked long into my eyes with an expression both persuasively eloquent and strong-willed in her beautiful, agitated face. I must believe, she at last assured me with the quick movement of her head, with which she always emphasized her words, that concerning ourselves she knew a thousand times better than any doctor what God would have, and in this we ought to obey God and not a doctor's human wisdom. And I was in many things so intensely simple-minded, that I could be made to believe anything.

People like the doctor, she said, had no idea what love was. Had I been strong and well, it would certainly have been God's will that she should have shared the good with me, and so it must just as much be His will that the same love should share my sorrow and sickness; but it was in this that Dr. K. – he evidently became more and more an object of hatred to her the longer she discussed him – thought differently from God. Besides, she believed so surely – and her voice here became wonderfully gentle and soft, almost a whisper – that just this, as we two were so fond of one another, would be a better cure for me than anything a doctor could invent. At any rate, she felt within herself that she would fall ill and give way to despair if I no longer cared for her, for had we not cared for each other as long as we could remember, and it was certainly too late to think of separating us.

One thing must now be settled – and at the thought her face assumed an expression of determined will, which reminded me of her father – and that was that, as soon as possible, she would confide everything about our engagement to her father. It ought, both for my sake and hers, to be no longer a secret. Her father was very fond of her, and, if need be, she would tell him seriously that it would be of no use either for him, or for anyone else – by this she meant her mother – to try any longer to get a doctor to separate us by guile.

Anything like a brotherly and sisterly love between us, as she, with scornful contempt in her look, expressed it, she would not hear of, least of all now, and as if entirely to dispel this idea, she stood upright before me, and asked me, as she looked with passionate eagerness into my face, to say that we still were, and in spite of everything and everybody always should remain, faithfully betrothed, even if I never became so well that we could marry here on earth – and to give her my kiss upon it.

I took her in my arms, and kissed her warmly and passionately once, twice, three times, until she freed herself.

While she was speaking it had dawned upon me that she, with her strong, healthy, loving nature, had fought the fight for us both and for a right that could not, perhaps, be proved in words, but the sanctity of which, I felt, was beyond all artificial proof.

Susanna now again belonged to me in another, truer, and more real way than I had ever dreamt of or suspected, as I comprehended that everything that could be called chivalrous sacrifice on my side only lay lower than our love, was even simply an unworthy offence to it. In true love the cross is borne by both the lovers, and the one who "chivalrously" wishes to bear it alone, only cheats the other of part of his best possession.

An hour after this interview with Susanna, which ended in renewed vows and promises, I was sitting in the stern of our ten-oared boat, together with my father and the two Martinezes, in the dark winter evening, while the moon was sailing behind a countless number of little grey clouds.

Father sat in silence and steered, while the men rowed against a rather stiff breeze which blew up the Sound, so that we might get the wind in our sails the rest of the way.

I quietly thought over everything that had passed during this short visit, and felt infinitely happy.

We reached home late at night. I tried to keep awake and to think about Susanna and all she had said to me, but I slept like a log, and awoke with a feeling of such health, happiness, and joy, as only those know to whose lot it has fallen to sleep the sleep of the really happy. And thus it was every night. I fell asleep before my prayers were ended, sang in the morning, and felt light-hearted almost to reckless gaiety, happy and ready for work the whole day long.

This proved how truly Susanna had said that our love would become to me a spring of health, better than any doctor's human wisdom could devise.

# Chapter X
## THE STORM

It was late in the afternoon of the Saturday after Twelfth Night that the terrible two days' storm began, which is still spoken of by many as one of the most violent that has visited Lofoten within the memory of man.

It was fortunate that the fishing had not yet begun – the storm raged with grey sky, sleet, and tremendous seas from the southwest right up the West Fjord – or perhaps as large a number of wrecks might have been heard of as in the famous storm of 1849, when in one day several hundred boats were lost. This time only a few boats were wrecked on their way to the fishing, and several yachts and a couple of larger vessels were stranded.

The storm increased during the night; we could feel how the house yielded at each burst, groaning at every joist, and we all sat up and watched with lights, as if by silent agreement.

All window-shutters, doors, and openings were carefully closed. The tiles rattled noisily at each gust, so that we were afraid the roof would be broken in, and the wind in the chimney made a deep, weird, growling noise, which in the fiercest attacks on the house sounded like a loud, horrible monster voice out in the night, sometimes almost like a wild cry of distress.

We sat in the sitting room in a silence that was only now and then broken by some remark about the weather, or when one or other of the men came in from making the round of the house to see how things were going on.

My father sat in restless anxiety about the storehouse, and about his yacht lying down in the bay, which, because of the heavy seas which came in, in spite of the harbor's good position, had been trebly moored in the afternoon. I saw him several times fold his hands as if in prayer, and then, as if cheered, walk up and down the room for a while, until anxiety again overcame him, and he sat down looking straight before him, gloomy and pale as before.

The storm rather increased than abated. Once we heard a dull thud, which might well have come from the storehouse. I saw drops of perspiration standing on my father's forehead, and was deeply pained to see his anguish of mind, without being able to do anything to help him.

A little while after he went out into the office with a candle and came back with an old large-type prayer-book, in which he turned to a prayer and a hymn to be sung during a storm at sea.

All the servants without being called, gathered in the parlor for family worship.

My father sat with the prayer-book in his great rough hands, which he had folded on the table before him, between the two candles. First he read the prayer, and then sang all the verses of the hymn, while those of us who knew the tune joined by degrees in the refrain. It was altogether as if we were holding prayers in a ship's cabin while the vessel was in danger, and my father must have had the idea from some such scene in his hard youth. During prayers we all thought the storm abated a little, and that it only began again after they were ended.

We found the elder Martinez on his knees by his bedside, perpetually crossing himself before a crucifix. He had less reason for anxiety than we, for his brig lay with extra moorings under land in a little creek sheltered from the wind and waves. He very much regretted now, however, that he had not gone on board to his son and the men.

Towards morning the storm abated a little, and, tired as we were, we went to bed, while two of the servants still sat up.

It was about ten o'clock in the morning, when it began to grow light, that we could first see the destruction done. Several hundred tiles from the house roof lay spread over the yard, part of the outer paneling of the wall on the windward side was torn away, and the end of the pier lay on one side down in the sea, a couple of piles having been displaced by the waves. The storehouse, too, had suffered some damage.

Our yacht, however, was most evidently in danger. Two of her ropes had given way, the anchors having lost their hold, and everything now depended upon the third and longest rope, which was fastened to the mooring ring on the rock at the mouth of the bay. There was only the ship's dog on board, a large white poodle, which stood with its fore-paws on the stern bulwarks and barked, without our being able to hear a sound in the wind, while the waves washed over the yacht's bows.

The situation was desperate, for the long rope was stretched as tight as a violin string, and the middle of it scarcely touched the water. It was blowing so hard, too, that a man could hardly stand upright, but was obliged to creep along the clean-swept snow-field, so that there could be no thought of helping.

I had crept up the hill at the back of the house, and stood in the shelter of a rocky knoll, from which I could see both out over the sea and down into the bay.

West Fjord on this wintry day lay as if covered with a silvery grey smoke from the spray that was driving across the sea. Beneath the cliffs the waves came in like great, green, foam-topped mountains, breaking on the shore with a noise like thunder, and then retreating an immense distance, leaving a long stretch of dry beach.

At one place, where a rock went perpendicularly down to the sea, a great, broad jet of spray was sent straight up every time a wave broke, and was driven in over the land by the wind like smoke. At another place the waves stormed in a Titanic way a sloping rock, which lay, now in foam, now high and dry, and I saw a poor exhausted gull, which had probably got out from its mountain cliff into the wind, fighting and battling in it, often with its wings almost twisted.

In anxious suspense I watched the yacht down in the bay. To my astonishment, I saw a man on board, and recognized the stalwart Jens, who had ventured out with one of the men, from the windward side, in a six-oared boat. After a short stay on board he stepped down alone into the boat with a rope round his waist, and began the dangerous work of hauling the boat against the waves, along the tight land-rope, out towards the rock.

I expected every instant that the boat would fill, and it seemed to me that the waves washed in several times. As the boat slowly worked its way along, father and all the servants followed it anxiously with their eyes, from the beach.

When Jens had got up on to the rock, over which the waves washed one after another, so that he often stood in water up to his knees, he secured the boat, and began to haul in the line, drawing after it through the water a thick cable, which the man on board was paying out gradually. He had just begun to fasten it to the mooring ring, and had only the last two knots in the rope to make, when we all became aware of three tremendous waves that would infallibly break over the rock.

Jens's life was evidently in danger, and the yacht too, which, with her one overstrained rope, would scarcely be able to bear the pressure.

I saw French Martina, his *fiancée,* clasp her hands above her head and run out into the surf, almost as if she thought of throwing herself into the water to go to him, and I think that not one of the others looking on dared to draw breath.

It appeared that Jens had noticed the danger himself; he hastened down to the boat, in which he could still shelter himself, but it was only to take up from it the line, which he calmly wound several times round his body and through the mooring ring, as he could no longer rely upon his own giant strength.

He had scarcely completed these preparations, when the first wave, which he faced with bent head, broke right over him and the rock. The interval before the second came he employed in making another knot in the land-rope.

Again came a wave, and again Jens stood firm, and he now made the final knot in the rope that saved the yacht.

He had now made trial of what the force of a wave could be. He threw the line from his back up round his great broad shoulders, turned his strong pale face towards our house for a moment, as if it were quite possible that he was now bidding it farewell, and bent his head towards the third and last wave, which was advancing with a foaming crest, as usual, larger than its two predecessors.

When the wave had broken in foam, and gone by, no Jens stood on the rock.

I ran down in horror to the others. When I got there, they had recovered, besides the boat, which had been torn from the rock, the apparently lifeless body of Jens, and were now carrying it to the house.

The wave had dragged him along, the line that he had round his shoulders having slipped up to his neck, and taken clothes and skin with it. He now lay unconscious from the pressure of the water, and with one arm, torn and bleeding from the line, in a twisted position: it was laid bare, at one place even to the bone.

Father walked with a pale face and supported him while they carried him up and put him to bed.

When he recovered consciousness, he began spitting blood, and had a difficulty in speaking; but father, who examined his chest, said joyfully that there was no danger.

By this exploit of saving the yacht Jens became famed as a hero far and wide; from that day forward, he was one of my father's trusted men, and in the following summer he and French Martina were married.

# *Chapter XI*
## CONCLUSION

I can now calmly write down the little, for me so much, that remains to be told – for many years it would have been impossible.

The storm lasted from Saturday midday until Sunday night, when towards morning the wind gradually subsided into complete stillness, although the sea continued restless.

The same day, Monday, at midday, there landed at the parsonage landing-place, not the minister's white house-boat, that was expected home, but an ordinary tarred, ten-oared boat, with a number of people in it.

From it four of the men slowly bore a burden between them up to the house, while a big man and a little woman went, bowed down, hand in hand, after them. It was the minister and his wife.

I understood at once what had happened, and my heart cried with despair.

The dreadful message, which came to us directly after, told me nothing new – it only confirmed my belief that it was the minister's daughter Susanna they had borne up.

The parsonage boat had been only a little more than three-quarters of a mile away from home that Saturday morning when the storm came on so suddenly. A "windfall" had come down with terrible force from the mountains into the Sound, and had capsized the boat, which was not far from land.

The minister had quickly helped his wife up on to the boat, and the men held on round the edge, while they drifted before the wind the short distance in to the shore. But he searched in vain for his child, to find her and save her.

With the sea seething round the boat, the strong man three times in his despair let go his hold in order to swim to the place where he imagined he saw her in the water. He was going to try again, but his wife, in great distress, begged his men to hinder him, and they did so.

They said afterwards that they saw drops of perspiration running down the minister's forehead, as he lay there on the boat in the wintry-cold sea, and that they believed he even thought of purposely letting go his hold that he might follow his daughter.

Too late they found out that Susanna was under the boat. She had become entangled in a rope, so that she could not rise to the surface.

Her death had at any rate been quick and painless.

The whole of Saturday and Sunday, while the storm lasted, they were compelled to lie weather-bound at a peasant's house in the neighborhood, where the minister's wife had kept her bed from exhaustion and grief.

The minister had sat nearly the whole time in the large parlor where they had laid Susanna, and talked with his God; and on Monday morning, when they were to go home, he was resigned and cairn, arranged everything, and comforted his poor, weeping wife.

I had lain in dumb, despairing sorrow the whole afternoon and throughout the long night, and determined to go the next day and see Susanna for the last time.

Early in the forenoon, the minister unexpectedly entered our parlor, and asked to speak to my father. He looked pale and solemn as he sat on the sofa, with his stick in front of him, and waited.

When my father came in at the door, the minister rose and took his hand, while the tears stood in his eyes.

After a pause, as if to recover himself, he said that my father saw before him an unhappy but humble man, whom God had to chasten severely before his will would bend to Him. He wanted now, because of his unhappiness, to ask my father not to deny him his old friendship any longer.

Of the matter that had caused the estrangement he would not now speak; he had acted to the best of his judgment. There was, however, something else which now lay on his heart, and here he put his hand on my shoulder and drew me affectionately to him, as he once more sat down on the sofa.

His daughter Susanna, he continued, sighing at the name, a few days before God took her to Himself, had admitted him into her confidence, and told him that she had loved me from the time she was a child, and that we two had already given each other our promise, with the intention of telling our parents when I became a student.

At first he had been strongly opposed to the engagement for many reasons, first and foremost my health and our youth. But Susanna had shown such intense earnestness in the matter and expressed such determined will, that, knowing her nature, it became clear to him that this affection had been growing for many years and could not now be rooted up. And it was now the greatest comfort he had in the midst of his sorrow, that the same morning on which they were to start on their ill-fated journey home, he had given in, and had also promised to use his influence in getting my father to give his consent.

Instead of this he now stood without a daughter, and only as one bringing tidings that the disaster had fallen on my father's house too, and struck his only child. He wished, he hoped with my father's permission, henceforth to regard me as his son.

My father sat a long time, surprised and pale; he seemed to have great difficulty in taking in what was said.

At last he rose and in silence gave his hand to the minister. Then he laid it on my shoulder so that I felt its pressure, looked into my eyes and said, in a low, wonderfully gentle voice:

"The Lord be with you, my son! Sorrow has visited you young; only, do not be weak in bearing it!"

He was going out to leave us alone together, but bethought himself in the doorway, and said that I had better go with the minister and take a last farewell of Susanna.

A little later the minister and I were walking side by side along the road. Our relations had now become confidential, and to comfort me he told me all that Susanna had said to induce him to consent. She knew, thank God, he concluded with a sigh of relief, that she had in her father a friend in whom she could confide in the hour of need.

The minister led me into the room with its drawn blinds; he stood for a moment by the bier, then the tears fell like rain down his broad, strong face, and he turned and went out.

She lay there in her maidenly white dress. They had twined a wreath of green leaves with white flowers about her head, and for a moment I saw again the vision I had at the ball. The delicate hands now lay meekly folded upon her breast, and on the engagement finger I recognized with tears my own old bronze ring with the purple glass stones in it, that she had worn from the moment she had obtained her father's consent. The expression of the mouth, so energetic in life, was transformed in death into a quiet, happy smile, in which her beautiful delicate face, with its broad pure marble brow shone with a heavenly radiance; she lay in such innocent security, as if she now knew the secret of true love's victory over everything here on earth, and was only gone in advance, with white wings on her shoulders, to teach it to me, since God had not allowed her to share the burden of my cross here below.

When I noticed that they wanted me to go, I silently repeated "Our Father" over her as a last farewell, pressed one gentle kiss upon her brow, then one upon her mouth, and one upon her folded hands where the bronze ring was, and went out without looking back.

Two days after, I followed Susanna's remains to the grave.

One sunshiny day in winter, when I as usual visited the place where she rested in the churchyard, the snow had drifted over her grave. It lay pure and dazzlingly white, with the fine upper edge like translucent marble in the sunlight.

I took this to mean that Susanna would have me think of her in her shining bridal dress before God, in order to give me courage to go my lonely way through life, and not to fear that the hardest of all trials – even insanity, if it came and enthralled me in its confusion – could separate us.

Late in the summer, when I was to go south by the steamer, together with the minister and his wife, who had both, in a short time, aged perceptibly, and who were now moving to a southern parish, I went for the last time to take leave of my sorrowful friend, the clerk.

He played the beautiful, joyful, beloved piece again for me, which he had composed when he was twenty, and which I had thought suited Susanna and me so well, and now he played the continuation too – it was wonderfully touching and sad, but with comfort in it, like a psalm.

Thus ends a poor, delicate Nordlander's simple story; for to tell how, with my father's help, I became a student with *"laud"** – he died the same year that I passed my *Examen artium,* a respected but ruined man – and how I afterwards became something of a literary man, a private tutor and a master in a school, is only to relate the outward circumstances of a monotonous life, whose thoughts all dwell in the past.

My love for Susanna has, as she said to me with such confidence,

* There are four grades in the Academic Degrees Examination – viz., *laudabilis præ ceteris, laudabilis, haud illaudabilis,* and *non-contemnendus.*

been the fountain of health that saved me from the worst madness. When restlessness came over me, and I roamed about aimlessly in field and forest, it always came to a crisis, when I saw her, in her white dress, floating by a little way off, or sometimes even coming gently towards me; then the danger was over for the time.

During the last two years, when I have been getting worse, I have not been fortunate enough to see her, and have had a dreary time, often as if the darkness were closing helplessly round me.

But not long ago, as I lay ill in my garret, Susanna came one night, when the full moon was shining, up to the bed, in her white bridal dress, with a wreath upon her beautiful hair, and beckoned to me with the hand that bore the ring. I know she came to bring me the glad tidings that I shall soon go hence and see again the love of my youth.

www.ingramcontent.com/pod-product-compliance
Lightning Source LLC
Chambersburg PA
CBHW030419310726
48979CB00007B/1110

*9781598182941*